CAROLS

AND CRUSHES

CAROLS AND CRUSHES

Natalie Blitt

SCHOLASTIC INC.

ISBN 978-1-338-08780-2

10 9 8 7 6 5 4   20 21 22 23

Printed in the U.S.A.   40

First printing 2016

Book design by Jennifer Rinaldi

FOR KATIE D'ANJOU

in thanks for many years of sharing

your Christmas celebrations with me

Chapter One

It's 11:48 p.m. and I can't sleep.

This is a big problem.

I've tried deep breaths. I've tried counting to two hundred and counting backward from two hundred (I couldn't remember which one was supposed to be good for falling asleep). I've tried reading. I've tried reading really, really boring books.

But nothing is working. My heart is racing and I truly now understand what it means to have ants in your pants, because I can't stop moving.

I side-eye the paper that hangs above my desk. Even in the pitch-black of my room, I can make out the list of songs we will be preparing for the holiday concert.

Tomorrow is the first day back to school after Thanksgiving break. It's the day we will officially start rehearsing for the concert. And Mrs. Hamilton, the teacher who heads up our school chorus, will announce how the soloists will be chosen this year.

Don't think about tomorrow, I tell myself.

I can't think about how excited I am to finally *be* in the middle school holiday concert, the same one I attended wide-eyed every year when I was in elementary school.

I can't think about what it might feel like if I get picked to be a soloist.

Even though, clearly, I can't think of anything else.

I flip over so I have my back to the song list tacked above my desk. This way I'm staring through the window at the dark sky, inky black with only a smattering of stars.

Silent night. Holy night.

I can't help it. Even looking at the sky makes me think of the concert and Christmas carols and . . .

This is ridiculous.

I climb out of bed and grab the sheet of paper that has been taunting me since I got into bed two hours and twelve minutes ago. I'll look over the list of carols one more time, and then I'll be able to fall asleep.

- *Silent Night*
- *Have Yourself a Merry Little Christmas*
- *Walking in a Winter Wonderland*
- *It's the Most Wonderful Time of the Year*
- *Let It Snow*
- *All I Want for Christmas Is You*

Pure poetry!

I visualize myself onstage, the rest of the chorus standing behind me. I can hear the restlessness in the air, the faint squeaking of chairs in the audience, the unwrapping of candies from noisy cellophane. My heart beats hard in my chest and my hands are clammy. But when my turn comes, I take a breath and the notes drift out of my mouth. The notes are quiet at first, maybe even a little too quiet. The crowd leans forward, as if they know something big is coming.

And then my voice takes root, and I can feel it echoing through my body, through my chest, vibrating my vocal cords, and then bellowing out as the sweetest sound.

The crowd remains quiet. Wrappers have been forgotten, children no longer cause chairs to squeak.

The chorus joins me when it comes to the *pa-rum-pum-pum-pums*, while the beatboxers mimic the sound of the drums, and it's magical.

We are singing "The Little Drummer Boy." Even though it's not on the list, it's my favorite carol. The beating of the drum fills my heart, and my whole body vibrates with the energy.

It's now time for Eric Sosland to step up and join me in

the solo. He takes my hand and I feel the energy shooting between the two of us. The audience is mesmerized. My mom has a tear in her eye.

And this is just the first song. Wait until they hear me and Eric do "All I Want for Christmas Is You." They may need to cancel all further concerts because nobody will be able to compete with this year's.

The door creaking open makes me jump at least a foot and yelp. Loudly.

"Shhhh," my sister, Sadie, begs, closing the door behind her. "You'll wake up Mom and Dad."

The list of songs is now clutched in my hand, pressed against my racing heart. "You scared me!"

"Sorry!" she says as she walks quietly over to my bed. "I heard you moving around, so I knew you were awake."

"I could have been sleepwalking," I growl.

Sadie rolls her eyes. Did I roll my eyes when I was seven? I can't even imagine. I think I spent all my time reading horse books and fairy tales.

Which I wouldn't say out loud to Sadie. I feel a flash of guilt. Sadie has trouble with reading.

And also, apparently, with sleeping. (That makes two of us.)

My sister plops onto my bed and scootches over to the window. "Hey, Charlie?" she says.

"Yeah?" I answer, making room for her.

"When are you going to put up your decorations?"

I pretend for a moment not to know exactly what she's talking about, but she's no dummy. "Mom said not until December tenth."

"Why?"

"I dunno." I sigh. Mom and I got into an epic throw-down fight after Halloween when I brought down the Christmas boxes from the attic. She said we had to wait until at least after Thanksgiving. Then, this past weekend was Thanksgiving, and Mom pushed the date into December. Typical.

I love Christmas. I always have. I love everything about the whole holiday season: the decorations, the songs (of course), the movies, the treats (what's better than hot cocoa with whipped cream?). I even love winter: the snow and the cold and the big boots and thick sweaters I get to wear.

People sometimes say I love Christmas so much because my name is Charlotte—Charlie—Dickens. Just like Charles Dickens, the author of *A Christmas Carol.* When my parents named me, though, they weren't thinking of *A Christmas Carol.* My dad's last name happens to be Dickens, and he and Mom thought it would be clever to name their daughter after an author they both love. I'm worried that maybe they were thinking of other Charles Dickens books, like *Oliver Twist* (which is a super-depressing story) or *A Tale of Two Cities* (which I haven't read but I bet is depressing, too) instead of *A Christmas Carol.*

A Christmas Carol is not depressing. Nothing about the holidays can be, really.

But the rest of the Dickens family is not into the holidays the way I am. I mean, we get a tree (a small one) and exchange presents on December 25. But my parents only put up the tree the day before and then take it down as quickly as possible (Mom complains about all the pine needles falling everywhere). And my parents prefer giving "experiences" instead of actual wrapped gifts—things like cards promising a family trip. They think it's more meaningful that way and avoids the "commercialism" of the holidays. I get that, but sometimes I wouldn't mind a big box to unwrap.

And if it were up to me, Christmas would be a two-month-long celebration, not a one-day thing.

I shake my head, pushing Christmas out of my thoughts and focusing on my little sister.

"Sadie, you're supposed to be asleep." I tack the song list back up on my bulletin board and slip back under the covers. For a long time, Sadie and I slept in the same room, but when I turned twelve, I put my foot down and insisted I needed my own space. Which means that I'm now sleeping in what used to be the guest room and whenever actual guests come, I have to go back to my bunk bed with Sadie. Which is also why Mom is picky about how messy my room can get, *and* about the idea of decorations. Apparently, it doesn't feel like a guest room if there are Christmas lights framing the window, or wreaths and sprigs of holly all over the place.

I try not to argue because I did technically agree to these conditions. However, I don't understand why my older brother, Jed, doesn't need to give up *his* room to guests and bunk up with Sadie. Though I can't imagine Jed being able to remove all the sports stickers and posters that decorate every available inch of his wall space.

"I can't sleep," Sadie admits. She's staring out the window, so I can't entirely see her face. But her voice is sad, which is the only reason I don't say: *Thanks for that, Captain Obvious.*

"Are you worried about something?" I ask. I lie back in my bed, pulling my knees up to my chest. Now I'm actually a little tired.

"I'm supposed to meet with the reading person tomorrow," Sadie says. Her words are so quiet that I almost miss them.

"But Mom said you shouldn't worry about it. The reading

specialist's job is just to figure out what you need help with so that they can—"

"I don't need help!" Sadie says, probably a little louder than she'd intended to. "The reading lady is going to tell me I'm dumb and that I'll have to keep reading these dumb little kid books for the rest of my life. And—"

"Sadie, that's not what's going to happen."

"But what if it does?"

I'm suddenly exhausted. I understand Sadie's tendency to worry. I'm worried, too—about the holiday concert.

"Do you want to come snuggle with me?" I ask, and almost before the words are out, Sadie's on the move. I open my arms and Sadie clambers in close, and I smooth down her hair, which is the same dark-blond shade as mine.

While it helps that I have a full-size bed, I also know that within a second of falling asleep, Sadie's little body will be covering the entire mattress.

Tomorrow, I think as I yawn. *Tomorrow I'll find out exactly what's happening with the concert.*

Chapter Two

Eleanor Roosevelt Middle School is a crazy mess of a school at any time. But this morning's snowstorm didn't help at all. And it wasn't the kind of pretty snowstorm that I love. It was wet and gray and slushy. You can't even go sledding on it; it just melts and freezes and goes dark and gross.

I meet my best friend, Renee Levine, in the hallway by our lockers, both of us dripping in our parkas and soggy snow boots. Everyone pushes and elbows in the crowd around us.

All the elementary schools in the district feed into our one tiny middle school. There's been talk about expanding the building, but according to my dad, nobody can agree on where the money should come from. So the school just keeps adding trailers when they run out of classrooms.

Which is a pain when it's anything but gorgeous outside.

"I hear a West Side bus got stuck and they had to send a new bus," Renee informs me as we put our parkas away. "And two South Side buses were really late to start their routes."

Renee always knows the gossip since her aunt works in the office and coordinates our elaborate busing system.

"Is the West Side bus here yet?"

It seems impossible that three buses are missing; the hallways are completely filled with wet jackets and boots.

"Nope. And yes, it was Eric's bus."

That's the thing about best friends, they know what you're really asking.

"That's not what I was asking," I lie.

"Oh?" Her eyebrows go up. Renee's hair is as thick and curly as mine is thin and straight. We frequently argue about which sucks more, though I still maintain that Renee only argues to make me feel better. Because curly hair is way better than wispy hair. Except, when Renee raises her eyebrows, the curls coming down from her forehead blend in with her brows and it makes her look like her hairline starts just above her eyes.

It always makes me laugh. In a good way.

"I'm sorry," she fake apologizes with a wry smile. "I just figured that since you didn't ask about the South Side buses, you were concerned about someone on the West Side bus. And given that you keep staring at Eric's locker, I guessed it was him."

I snort. I like to think Renee's the only one who knows about my epic crush on Eric Sosland, the crush that started in fourth grade when we were put in the same "family unit" for our *Mayflower* project. Three weeks of pretending to be

Eric's wife for social studies class and . . . Well, it sounds dumb, but I think it changed something between us.

Not that he and I have ever talked about it.

Or talked much at all . . .

"It's cold outside," I mutter. "I was concerned about everyone getting to school."

Renee laughs as she bangs her locker shut. "Well, the bigger issue is that they're going to have to rearrange stuff today so that nobody is missing classes because of the buses. They're even talking about canceling the lunch period and having classes meet in the cafeteria."

I pull my hair up into an elastic on top of my head and twist it a few times until it becomes a makeshift bun. Then I sling the long strap of my briefcase bag over my shoulder.

While I love my high boots and big sweaters, my brown leather briefcase is my absolutely favorite possession. My grandmother brought it back for me from Italy when she and my grandfather went last year. I know my parents thought it was a bit much, and they dropped some hints that I should save it for when I'm in high school. Or college. As if I could wait that long. They argued that it could get lost or ruined, but they've now admitted how wrong they were. This bag is my precious. Especially since it contains my journals and my favorite pens. And it goes perfectly with every outfit.

Or rather, I select outfits based on whether they'd go nicely with the bag.

"Wait, but what about chorus?" I ask Renee. Because chorus is an elective, it's held during lunch. Sports teams get the after-school times and chorus gets lunch. Not that there's any preferential treatment going on.

They can't cancel chorus today. They just can't.

"Not sure." Renee is in chorus, too, but it's not an obsession for her like it is for me. At first she wasn't going to even sign up for it, but I promised her it would be totally fun, and so far she seems okay with it.

Someone's wet scarf hits me in the face as I shut my locker. *Please don't cancel chorus*, I beg the universe. *Please, please, please.*

Apparently someone is listening to me. Or at least somewhat listening. Chorus is still on, but it's shortened to a half-class. Which kind of bites, but it's enough time for Mrs. Hamilton to tell us what's going on with the concert.

Except she's not there.

For the first few minutes, there was excited chatter and now . . . we're all nervous. Because Mrs. Hamilton is never ten minutes late for anything. If this were any other class, we would have walked out. But this is chorus. And it's already shortened. Why would Mrs. Hamilton waste any of the little time we have?

"What do you think is happening?" I mumble to Renee without looking at her. Instead, I'm staring across the room, not at the door where Mrs. Hamilton might walk through nor at the clock, but rather at Eric. He looks like he always does: tall, with brown skin, and close-cropped curly dark hair. And of course, he's ridiculously cute. But he looks nervous, and I know he's as anxious as I am to hear about the concert.

That's one of the things that makes it clear that Eric and I are a good match: We both love to sing. Eric's one of the best boy singers in chorus, so he's practically a shoo-in for a solo. And if I got one of the other two solos, that would be . . .

Well, it would literally be a dream come true since I actually dream about it on a regular basis.

When the door swings open, we all quiet down. Except it's not Mrs. Hamilton who walks in but the vice principal, Mr. McHenry. When he steps into the classroom, the room goes from quiet to still.

I crane my neck to see Mrs. Hamilton, but the door shuts behind Mr. McHenry.

Uh-oh.

Mr. McHenry gives us all a tight-lipped smile and then sits on the front edge of Mrs. Hamilton's desk. He takes a deep breath and lets it out.

"So I have good news and bad news," he starts.

I hope he doesn't make us vote as a class on which one we want to hear first. I know he's trying to be the "cool" vice principal, with his hipster glasses and sneakers. He never wears suits like the principal wears. But I wish he would just get to the point.

"The good news," he goes on—phew, "is that Mrs. Hamilton gave birth to a very healthy baby boy on Thanksgiving Day."

"Wait, I thought she wasn't due until Christmas Day?" asks Matthew Yee, who is captain of the middle school basketball team. Matthew is also one of the most popular kids in the grade. Everyone seems to like him.

Except maybe me. Because there's something really irritating about how everybody fawns all over him. I'm not sure why he needed to add chorus to the mix of all his extracurriculars. Between his big group of friends and his basketball schedule, I don't get his interest in singing. It seems fake.

"Maybe the baby got Christmas and Thanksgiving mixed up," Kyle says. He's one of Matthew's popular friends in chorus, and I scowl at the two of them. I want to just tell them to be quiet but, luckily, Mr. McHenry does it for me. With a look.

I like this guy more already.

"The baby was born prematurely, but so far, that doesn't seem to have caused any problems," Mr. McHenry explains. "He's already out of the NICU, and they're bringing him home either Tuesday or Wednesday."

Okay. So that's the bad news. We have to wait a bit . . .

"All this of course means that Mrs. Hamilton has begun her maternity leave early and will be gone until the beginning of next semester. And sadly, that brings me to the bad news."

I freeze.

"The holiday concert has really been Mrs. Hamilton's project since the beginning," Mr. McHenry continues. "If we'd known earlier that she would be leaving before the concert, we could have found someone from the community to take it over. But at this point, it's just too late."

Oh no. No. No.

"I spoke with Mrs. Hamilton about it this morning as we tried to figure out another way, but neither of us could," Mr. McHenry goes on solemnly, while my heart sinks. "If it were a couple of more weeks closer to the concert, Mrs. Hamilton said she could have come to school for a few hours, but only once or twice. And certainly not right now with a newborn who is just out of the NICU. I'm very sad to say that we're going to have to cancel the holiday concert . . ."

The rest of his words get drowned out by the noise of everyone reacting at once.

Everyone except me. Because for the life of me, I can't make a sound.

They can't cancel the concert.

They can't.

It's too important.

It's a tradition.

Mr. McHenry is trying hard, answering all the questions he can as I stare at the clock, watching the minute hand slowly round to the top of the hour when the lunch period will be over, and chorus will be done.

Eric speaks up. "Mr. McHenry? I know you and Mrs. Hamilton have discussed all the possible plans, but I wonder if I might suggest a different one?"

Oh gosh. Please let him have some brilliant plan. I swivel to face him. *Please, Eric. Please.*

"Go ahead." Mr. McHenry's voice is even, but it's evident that his patience is waning.

"I know that Mrs. Hamilton was really excited for the concert, as we all were," Eric continues, and I nod at him even though he can't see me. "And I know that she would want us to try anything possible to make the concert happen because it's an important tradition at the school."

I'm holding my breath, daring to feel hopeful.

"Mrs. Hamilton has already given us a list of carols for the show," Eric goes on, "so the only thing left to do is rehearse, and then pick the soloists. Is there another teacher who could supervise this time period and we'd—"

"There isn't another teacher," Mr. McHenry says curtly. "And the school rules state that any organized club or group at school needs a teacher present to use a room in the school. Believe me, I've asked every teacher who might have a spare period, but with it being the end of the term and report cards—"

"But wait!" I can't believe I'm suddenly speaking. And standing up. And that I've interrupted the vice principal. He isn't looking so cool-hipster right now. But this is our last chance. I have no choice but to be brave.

"Yes, Charlie?" Mr. McHenry says, looking at me over the top of his glasses.

I twist my hands together, my thoughts racing. "You said we couldn't rehearse on our own in the school and that there's nobody to supervise us."

"Yes."

Mr. McHenry does not appear to be happy. I don't glance around the room. All I can do is hope I have the support of the class.

"What if we didn't need to rehearse at school?" I suggest. "We're only sixteen people. We could rehearse at our houses. We have almost a month before the concert. If Mrs. Hamilton can come to school once or twice to help out in the week before the concert, that's all we'd need. And in the meantime, we'll organize it ourselves."

I take a deep breath. Mr. McHenry hasn't responded yet. But he also hasn't interrupted me to say no, either.

"We can practice by ourselves until we really, really know the songs, and then she can come in later and pick the soloists," I go on, figuring this is my last shot. "And even if Mrs. Hamilton can't come, we could find another judge to choose? We could even make it fun, like one of those sing-off competitions or something!"

I bite my lip. Maybe I've gone too far. There's chattering

again, but this time it's excited murmuring. I think the other students are agreeing with me! My heart soars. I glance at Renee, and she shoots me a thumbs-up.

But Mr. McHenry is staring at me, probably trying to figure out how he can shoot down the idea.

I need him not to do that. I have dreamt of singing onstage for as long as I can remember. I have dreamt of this concert. I need this concert.

Mr. McHenry opens and closes his mouth, as if he has more to say but thinks better of it. And when the bell rings, nobody moves. It's actually completely silent. Mr. McHenry looks to the ceiling for a moment, but it doesn't seem like he's rolling his eyes. It's like he's actually thinking about it.

Please. Please. Please. Please.

"I'm supposed to talk with Mrs. Hamilton this evening on another topic," he finally says. "Why don't I ask her for her thoughts? If the class is in fact committed to rehearsing, and we can find someone to figure out the soloist issue, maybe . . ."

His words are once again swallowed up by cheering and whoops in the room, but at least this time, I'm able to join in.

Mr. McHenry leaves the classroom, and the rest of us stand up to gather our things, everyone talking excitedly.

"You were awesome," Eric says as he passes by me.

I beam, feeling my face turn a good number of shades of red brighter than it is supposed to be. "It was your idea."

"No," he laughs. "My idea was to find another teacher."

"Well, it was great teamwork, then," I say, and his grin is wide.

I'm not sure what is causing more butterflies in my belly: the chance we might be able to save the concert or the conversation with Eric.

Chapter Three

We hear nothing for the rest of the day, which is to be expected, I guess. Though I had half hoped that Mr. McHenry would email Mrs. Hamilton immediately. But I get that he probably has other things to do. And that Mrs. Hamilton definitely does.

The next morning, I debate waiting outside Mr. McHenry's office and then "pretending" to run into him, but Renee tells me this is stalkerish behavior and that it won't help.

"But I could just walk back and forth in front of his office, so when he comes out, it'll be as if I just happened to be passing by?" I offer. Renee raises her eyebrows, and I shake my head. She doesn't really need to tell me how bad it sounds. But it's really difficult to make it through a full day at school with no word about the concert. It doesn't take long before all my optimistic vibes from yesterday are gone.

That evening, I consider telling my parents about the idea, to see if maybe they could call the school. Maybe they would even offer to host our practices. But something is clearly up, because Sadie's eyes are red and she's refusing to eat. Jed, my fifteen-year-old brother, doesn't seem to notice. He's just shoveling food in like he's in a timed eating race. I pick at my burger and mashed potatoes, but the tension at the table makes it hard to breathe, never mind talk about what's going on in school.

"Sadie," my mom tries when my sister refuses to even touch her food. "It's probably not even going to happen . . ."

Sadie's small body rotates away from the table, and in her new position, I can see that her lip is trembling. I glance up at Dad, who, along with Mom, stares at Sadie's curled form.

"Sades, it's just a test—" Dad says, but Sadie's eyes narrow.

"I took the test already. You said that was it. You said we'd have all the answers."

Right. The reading specialist meeting. It happened yesterday, but I'd been so consumed with the concert that I'd forgotten.

"Honey, they do. But we just need more information." Mom's voice is quiet but firm.

"I don't want to do it."

"Sadie, it's seriously no big deal," Jed pipes up, his words barely understandable through his mouthful. Ugh. "Everyone needs extra help in something. Remember how I needed to get extra sessions in basketball because I kept messing up my layup?"

"Your extra help came after school, where nobody saw you doing it," Sadie shoots back. "Everyone already makes fun of me because I can't read. Every time I have to go take the test with the learning specialist, the kids in my class snicker."

"They're just jealous," I say, and Sadie's eyes actually look almost hopeful. "They wish they could get out of class, too. Think of it like a special treat. Especially since Ms. Riley is so nice. If they laugh, just stick out your tongue."

Sadie gives me a half smile.

"Well, that might be pushing it," Dad interrupts. "Maybe you can just imagine sticking your tongue out."

Sadie glances over at me and I wink. I think it's totally fine if she sticks out her tongue.

As we're clearing dishes, I finally get a moment alone with Dad.

I'm about to bring up the concert, but he starts talking first.

"Charlie, thank you for stepping in with your sister," he says. "She really looks up to you. If we can just get through this testing period, I know that we'll figure out what Sadie needs."

I nod, rinsing off the plates one at a time. I don't get the point of rinsing off plates before they go into the dishwasher. When I'm a grown-up, I'm putting them straight in.

"Actually, Dad, I wanted to ask you about something . . ."

I let the words trail off, trying to figure out his mood. He shuts off the water and turns toward me, drying his hands on the towel. "What's up?"

My dad looks like the dictionary definition of an absent-minded professor, even though he isn't a professor but an accountant. His hair is always a little bit too shaggy, his button-down shirts are always slightly frayed, and his corduroys show their wear as their ridges flatten in front. Sometimes I wish he'd get a better haircut or wear sharper clothes, but his look is also part of what just makes him *Dad*, all rumpled and kindhearted.

"I wanted to ask—"

"Oh, good, Max, you're here," Mom interrupts, sailing into the room with her phone pressed against her ear. "I have Rosalyn from the testing center on the phone. She thinks that Sadie doesn't need to . . ."

My dad's focus switches from me to my mom. I wipe down the counters, trying to figure out whether I should stay and wait to talk to him, or forget about it.

Dad? I mouth, coming to stand behind Mom so I can get his attention. But evidently, that was the wrong thing, because he scowls. Maybe it's not at me but the discussion he's having with Mom?

Mom hands the phone to Dad and turns to me. "Charlie, if this is about Christmas decorations, I need you to wait until December tenth, as we agreed. If you want to decorate something at school, that's fine, but I'm just not ready for the house to be turned upside-down right now."

"It's not—" I begin.

"Honey, what we're discussing is important. Please don't

make me add another week for you to wait. Go up and do your homework."

I stare at the two of them, but they're back to talking with Rosalyn from the testing center. I'm sure once they're finished with her, they'll get on the phone with Jed's coach about whatever tournament is coming up, and then Sadie will need to be put to bed, and then Jed's homework will need to be checked and . . .

It's not even worth trying.

The next morning, before the first bell, Renee helps me decorate my locker.

It's not at all the same as decorating the house, but right now, I'll take it. I attach a paper snowflake to the front, and Renee rips off a piece of tape for the square of reindeer wrapping paper I saved from last year.

"Did you tell your parents about the concert?" Renee asks me, and I shake my head. My mom was so distracted when she came to say good night that I didn't bother bringing up the concert for fear that she would once again chide me.

"Too much going on with Sadie," I explain. "Plus, they're 'not ready' to deal with anything Christmas-y yet." I sigh.

"Sorry," Renee says. "I'm sure it will work out, though."

Renee has been my best friend forever, ever since she and her mom moved here from California when we were six. We share everything—heck, she knows more about me than anyone in the world. She certainly knows all about my crazy family. But there's one big difference between us: Renee manages to be happy most of the time. She doesn't care if she's the last one chosen for teams in gym class, or doesn't get invited to birthday parties. She moves on.

It kind of makes me crazy, as much as I love her.

"I was really born in the wrong family," I mutter, accepting the wrapping paper from Renee and carefully pasting it to my locker.

"You could be born into mine and then you wouldn't get Christmas at all," Renee reminds me.

"You celebrate Hanukkah!" I remind her. "You get pretty candles and eight nights of presents." I love going to Renee's house for Hanukkah, when her mom makes crispy potato pancakes and lights the menorah. Renee is an only child, so her house is always much calmer than mine.

"True," Renee says, cutting off more pieces of tape, this time so I can hang up a few garlands for a pop of color at the back of my locker. "Well, you know you have a standing invite to my house anytime."

"Thanks," I say just as the bell rings.

In homeroom, the morning announcements come in over the school loudspeaker. I half listen. *"Early dismissal today for eighth graders . . . third-floor boys' bathroom closed for repairs . . . blah blah blah . . ."*

And then I hear it:

"Mr. McHenry asks that the chorus meet at lunchtime today in the chorus room."

My heart leaps. Chorus is meeting today! That must

mean Mr. McHenry spoke to Mrs. Hamilton. This has to be a good thing . . . right?

At lunchtime, Renee and I meet at our lockers to drop off our morning textbooks and hurriedly discuss what the chorus meeting could mean.

"Hey, wanna walk over to the meeting together?"

I startle at the sound of Eric's voice behind us. He's never come to talk to me at my locker. I turn to Renee and widen my eyes.

"That sounds great," Renee says, correctly understanding that my ability to speak in full sentences might be hampered by Eric's presence. Yet another reason we need to save the concert: Despite all the things Eric and I have in common, chorus is the only class or activity we share. No chorus? No hanging out with Eric. Not that I've hung out with him before, but . . .

"Charlie, you coming?" Renee says. She and Eric evidently made it a few steps while I was lost in thought.

I slam my locker, hoping I didn't dislodge any of my decorations. "Absolutely."

The three of us head into the chorus room. I don't look at Renee, but I'm positive she's grinning at me. I cough to disguise the nervous laughter that's bubbling up.

Mr. McHenry is in the room waiting for us. I feel more nervous than ever.

"Thank you all for your patience," Mr. McHenry starts when we're all seated. "I've spoken with Mrs. Hamilton and she was happy to hear your plan, Charlie. The concert is back on!"

OMG.

There's mass pandemonium. Or at least as mass as you can get with sixteen kids. They cheer and clap. There are some thumps on my back, but I don't turn around. Instead, I stare dumbfounded at Mr. McHenry.

I saved the holiday concert. *I* saved the holiday concert.

"But she made a few changes," Mr. McHenry says, his voice rising over the din. "The concert will proceed without any solos. You can practice the selected songs on your own, and Mrs. Hamilton will come in to officially rehearse with you all the week before the concert."

The color drains from my face. No solos? Then it's just another group concert. And yes, I love singing as a group, but . . . but my dream . . .

My dream to finally stand out from the crowd. To have the audience—my parents—really see me, in the spotlight.

"Then what part of Charlie's plan did she like?" Eric's words cut through the panic currently ruling my thoughts.

"Well, leaving you to rehearse on your own is a leap of faith," Mr. McHenry explains. "Which is why she actually suggested that you be split into four groups of four, to make it a bit easier on you. *Also*, in lieu of individual solos, she would like to add a showcase performance. Each group of four will be responsible for picking five songs for a special quartet performance. They have to be songs not already on the main song list. Mrs. Hamilton has agreed that, barring any unforeseen circumstances, she'll come to school in three weeks to judge the groups. The best quartet will do the showcase performance at the concert."

Oh. My. A showcase performance? This could be better than a solo!

"I suggested to her that you be able to pick your own groups to work together," Mr. McHenry says, "but she thought it would be important to have a good range of voices in each quartet. As such, she assigned the teams herself."

He pulls out a sheet of paper from the folder he placed on Mrs. Hamilton's desk.

I still can't believe that my plan worked. Kind of. Maybe better than I had even thought possible? The noise of the room echoes inside my head, and I miss out on listening to the groupings until I hear my own name.

". . . Charlie Dickens, and Matthew Yee."

I sit up straight and glance around. Who else is in the group with us? But Mr. McHenry has moved on and is reading off a new group, and I can't very well interrupt him to ask. Ugh. I don't want to be in a group with Mr. Popularity, Matthew Yee.

It's not that Matthew has a bad voice. He doesn't. Although his is certainly not as good as Eric's. The problem is that Matthew knows he has a good voice. And that he's a great basketball player. And does well in school. And has tons of friends. Whenever he walks down the hall, he has a whole entourage. Not one of whom speaks to me when they pass.

Sometimes, Matthew says hello, though it's usually a full-name hello: *Hey, Charlie Dickens*, he'll say with a half smirk. Like he's the first one to think it's funny that my parents named me Charlie Dickens. *Trust me*, I want to yell, *I've heard all the dumb jokes already.*

But I never yell. I just glare. Which Renee claims looks more like a squint than anything else. So on top of everything, Matthew probably thinks I need glasses.

"Why aren't you happier?" Renee asks as the bell rings. "You look like someone ran over your dog."

"Did someone run over your dog?" Phoebe Miller asks from behind me. Phoebe is sweet, but I can't tell if she's joking or genuinely concerned, so I let Renee explain the concept of an expression to her. I wonder if Phoebe is jealous because she's not in a group with Matthew Yee—I've heard her and her best friend in chorus, Veronica Martinez, whispering about how they think Matthew is cute. I guess he *is* kind of cute, with his floppy black hair and bright dark eyes behind glasses. But I don't see him that way.

Anyway, maybe Phoebe *is* in Matthew's group. And mine. I would know if I had been listening!

"I thought you'd be super excited," Renee whispers to me as Phoebe gets up and leaves. Renee and I are the only ones left in the classroom now.

"Well, I'm excited the concert is back on," I say, getting to my feet.

"And what about the group?" Renee presses, her eyes sparkling.

"What about it?" I ask.

"We're in the same group," she says, her brow furrowed. At least I think it is, under all that curly hair.

I startle. "Wait, we are? That's great! So you, me, Matthew, and—"

She laughs. "Yes. You and me and Matthew and Eric."

Eric.

Eric?

I'm in the same group as Eric!

Chapter Four

I can't stop smiling as Renee and I head for the classroom door.

I'm in a group with Eric. And Renee. It couldn't be more perfect. And Matthew isn't the worst possible fourth. I won't even notice him because I'll be getting to sing with Eric after school.

Eeek.

Matthew and Eric stand in the hallway, evidently waiting for Renee and me.

"Good going, Dickens!" Matthew says, giving me a fist bump.

"It's really thanks to Eric in many ways." I'm staring at my boots and I hope nobody can see what is probably an enormous blush taking over my cheeks. I inherited my pale skin from Dad: When we blush, people can see it from miles away. The only thing worse is when we get a sunburn. That they can probably see from the International Space Station.

"Okay, yay, everyone," Renee says, ending the awkwardness. "So where should we meet? And when?"

"We can meet at my house," I say quickly, my eyes on Renee so that I don't blush. "I live pretty close to the school. We can walk from here."

Everyone nods but Renee. "Are you sure that's going to be okay with your parents?" she asks me knowingly.

"Of course," I fudge. "I'm sure it won't be a problem."

It has to be okay. And maybe after we rehearse, Eric and I can hang out. We can watch a movie and get some snacks . . .

"I have basketball usually two afternoons a week," Matthew says, staring at his phone.

I groan. I debate whether I should ask him if he really wants to continue with chorus since he already has so much on his plate. But I'm a little worried that with only three people, Mrs. Hamilton won't let us audition for the showcase.

"But I can do today," he adds, looking up.

I glance at Eric and Renee and they all nod.

"Okay," I say, standing tall and trying to quell the nervousness in my belly. "My house today, after school!"

"Let's meet by our lockers after the last bell and walk over together," Renee suggests.

The late bell rings, and we all scatter for our classes. It occurs to me that I *should* probably call home at some point to ask permission.

But I'm sure it'll be fine.

After school, the four of us—Renee, me, Matthew, and Eric (eep!)—walk in a group to my house.

My hands shake as I unlock the front door. I've never had a boy over to my house before. Let alone *two* boys. Let alone a boy I have a crush on!

Thankfully, the downstairs is empty. When I called earlier to ask if it was okay to bring friends over after school, Mom had reluctantly agreed, but she said she'd be up in Sadie's room working with her on reading.

The four of us gather in my living room, Renee and I sitting on the couch and the boys taking the floor.

"I guess we can start by rehearsing what's on the song list Mrs. Hamilton gave us," Matthew suggests, scrolling through his phone. "What were the songs again?"

"'Silent Night,' 'Have Yourself a Merry Little Christmas,' 'Walking in a Winter Wonderland,' 'It's the Most Wonderful Time of the Year,' 'Let It Snow,' and 'All I Want for Christmas Is You,'" I rattle off, not even pausing to think. It helps that I've sung the songs in bed ever since we received the song list.

"Wow," Eric says, and I turn to avoid everyone seeing the blush again. Except turning reveals all the family pictures on the mantle including . . . gah! Very, very embarrassing baby pictures of me.

Please don't let Eric notice them, I beg the universe.

"Why don't we start at the top?" Matthew asks.

Because we didn't know we'd be doing this, nobody has their music, so we try singing from memory.

We sound terrible.

"Maybe we should loosen up?" Renee suggests. "Like, do some of the warm-up exercises that Mrs. Hamilton makes us do."

We try those. We sound like barnyard animals.

"Can you guys keep it down a bit?" Mom has poked her head into the living room and she doesn't look happy. Though that might have to do with Sadie shouting upstairs. Or maybe we're singing louder to drown out Sadie's voice.

"Sure, Mrs. Dickens," Matthew says, and I can't tell if he's making fun of our name again. I glare-squint at him.

We try "Silent Night" again. We sound slightly better but we're tentative, our voices small. It's as if we're afraid of one another. When I raise my voice, Mom comes back to ask us to keep it down.

"Why don't you head outside?" she suggests.

"It's cold!" I protest. What kind of hospitality is this?

"Well, carolers always sing outside, so maybe it'll get you in the mood."

I roll my eyes. Mom smiles tightly.

"Fine, why don't you go down to the basement?" she suggests. "That way we won't bother you and you don't need to worry about being too loud."

Our basement is gross. It's still filled with old toys, boxes of old clothing to be donated, and Jed's used sports equipment.

"Mom, can't we just stay up here?" I whisper, stepping aside into the hallway to talk to her alone.

Mom sighs. "Well, maybe you'll check with me in advance next time before you invite your friends over, Charlie.

Sadie is supposed to be doing some practice tests, only she refuses to do it and I have twenty minutes before I need to take your brother to his basketball game in Hyatt. And your father is stuck with a client until five thirty. Before you showed up with your friends, I'd hoped I could leave Sadie with you while I drove Jed out there, and Dad could pick up pizza on his way home. But now she's freaking out and . . ."

"I can still stay home with her," I say, shrugging. "She can hang out while we rehearse."

"She needs to do her practice tests," Mom sighs. "I'd hoped to get them out of the way before you had to babysit, but all the disruption just got everything off schedule."

"Can I help?"

I whip around and see Eric standing behind us.

I soften. Of course Eric would offer to help. It's just the type of person he is.

Mom's eyes widen and she smiles. "Thank you . . ."

"Eric," he says, answering her silent question.

Oh no. In fourth and fifth grades, I used to talk about my crush on Eric all the time. What if she remembers? What if she says something embarrassing? I want to hide.

"Eric." The corners of her mouth inch up again, but it looks like I might be safe. "I appreciate the offer, but we're having a hard time with some test work that Sadie has to do and—"

"I'm not doing it!" Sadie bellows from upstairs. My ears hurt from the noise, and I can't believe Eric is listening to all this. It is so mortifying.

"Would it help if we rescheduled our rehearsal time?" he asks, and my mom nods.

"I'd love to have you kids practice here, but I just don't think it makes sense right now."

By now, Renee and Matthew have joined us in the hall-way, and I want to cry. Why can't this one thing work out for me? Why does it always have to be about Sadie and Jed?

"Maybe your mom was right about caroling outside," Matthew says. "Maybe next time, we could practice in Lincoln Square. It might be cold, but I think it would be nice to have other people listening. And it would bring some Christmas cheer."

I want to find a problem with his solution, but the truth is that I can't. It kind of makes sense.

I walk Eric, Matthew, and Renee to the front door, and they start putting on their jackets and hats and scarves. We agree to meet up on Friday after school.

"We should try to pick the five songs we want to present to Mrs. Hamilton," Eric says as he pulls on his woolen hat.

"I'll do that!" I volunteer. I love picking songs.

"And I'll help you," Matthew offers, which is surprising. I figure he hardly knows any holiday songs.

"Okay," I say because I'm too startled to protest. Then Matthew waves bye to us and heads out the door.

Suddenly, Eric turns to Renee.

"Why don't I walk you home?" he asks.

Um . . . what? It's still mostly light outside, which means there's really no good reason for Renee to need someone to walk her home.

Unless that someone just . . . wants to.

My heart sinks.

Please don't let Eric Sosland have a crush on Renee. Please, please, because that would be so awkward.

Nobody knows better than Renee how I feel about Eric.

And if he has a crush on her . . .

It means he doesn't like me.

Renee's head pivots to me, and her eyes are wide.

"Isn't that out of your way, Eric?" I ask.

"Nah," he says. "It's on the way to my bus stop, actually."

I glance at Renee. She could always say no. Or she could make an excuse to stay here with me. Or . . .

"Sure, it would be nice to have company," Renee finally says with a shrug.

I watch as Renee and Eric leave together.

I have a bad feeling about this.

* * *

"Do you like him?" I ask Renee for the fourth time the next morning. She's already apologized for not getting my subconscious message, but while I believe her, I also . . . don't. Which feels awful.

"He's a nice guy," she says, pulling her hair back with the elastic that she wears around her wrist. Renee always has an elastic around her wrist, because when she feels the need to put her hair up, it drives her crazy if she can't. Like crazy-crazy. I've seen it happen and it isn't pretty. And I get it, because that's how I react to overheating. Which is why Renee's mom carries extra bottles of water for me when she drives us anywhere.

"Nice guy like he's nice but no big deal, or nice guy like oooh, isn't he nice . . ." I change my voice for each alternative. I think I'm being pretty clear, but Renee stops and raises her eyebrows at me.

I giggle despite myself.

"Stop," she says. "Nice guy, full stop. He's your crush, not mine."

"Then why did you let him walk you home?"

The hallway around us is filled with the sounds of lockers slamming, but it isn't the noise that keeps Renee's answer from me. "I didn't think it was such a big deal," she finally answers, pulling the elastic high up in her ponytail. "If I had known that you'd see it as an ultimate betrayal, I never—"

"I didn't say—"

"You kind of did."

I close my eyes and lean back on my locker. "I thought this would be our big chance," I whisper, though it's not a revelation to Renee. She's known about my dream that the concert will show Eric how right we are together.

"It still can be. So he walked me home. We chatted about nothing in particular. You don't need to worry about me. I'm not here to take away your boyfriend."

I choke, whipping my head around to make sure no one heard her. "He's totally not my boyfriend," I whisper.

"Stop worrying," she says, "it's the holidays. And tomorrow we're going to go caroling in the street, which is totally your jam."

I hold on to that thought, but it doesn't bring much lightness.

Chapter Five

It seems like forever until the day is done. Maybe because our Spanish teacher insisted that we do worksheets in class, which always makes time slow to a stop.

To my shock, as I exit the classroom, I spot Matthew standing outside.

"Hey!" he says when I meet his gaze. "I was hoping to catch you."

His eyes twinkle as a slow smile overtakes his face. A smile directed at me? Weird.

"How did you know I'd be here?" I ask, though it's clearly not the most important question.

He shrugs one shoulder and appears almost sheepish. "I knew you took Advanced Spanish and my locker is down at North Bay, so I always see you walk past at the end of the day on Thursdays. So I figured, unless you were skipping, which seemed highly unlikely, you'd be coming out of this door at precisely this moment."

He stops talking and I realize with a start that he's waiting for me to say something, to carry on the next part of the conversation. But I'm still puzzling over the part where he said he sees me walk out of class. That he knows which class I'm in. It's like Matthew Yee is paying attention to me, which seems entirely impossible.

"Well, you're right on both counts," I finally get out. My face flushes when I replay the words that came out while my brain was on holiday.

"So we need to come up with a good list of carols for

tomorrow," Matthew says as we start to walk down the hall together. "Remember? The five songs?"

I nod.

"But I have a basketball game tonight," Matthew continues. "I don't know if you were planning to go to the game or not. I mean, not that you have to or anything . . . you probably have other things to do. But, if you were, or even really if you weren't, maybe we could head to the library and use one of those workrooms to come up with a plan? I can tell my mom that I'll walk home a little later, like right before I have to leave for the game. And if you were coming to the game, we could even give you a ride out there."

My head spins. "Um, I wasn't planning . . ." How can I say that the idea of going to a basketball game when I'm not forced to be there out of family loyalty gives me hives? "I'm not a basketball person," I finally say.

From the way his face drops, that was clearly not the right way to tell him.

"I mean, I have to go to a lot of my brother, Jed's, games, so I try to limit my time in the gym to . . ." I'm making zero sense. I can't even remember what the question was anymore.

But just as Matthew is about to reply, I hear a shout and I feel the smack of a basketball against my side. Is this payback for my comments?

"Oww," I cry out. I shift to the side of the hall, dropping my bag on the ground and rubbing my upper arm. Can a basketball break your arm? Is that even possible?

I rotate my arm as Matthew takes a step closer. "Mike, what were you thinking?" he calls over his shoulder. "Charlie, are you okay?"

"I'm fine." I bristle. I watch as Mike Hughes and a bunch of other basketball guys wave at us and shout apologies. Now that the pain in my arm is fading, I'm more annoyed that Matthew's whole popular posse had to witness the accident. "Maybe if you guys didn't play ball in the hallway, things like this wouldn't happen."

I don't mean to sound so crabby. I hear Mike hoot with laughter from across the hall. "Dude, she totally schooled you." He presses his lips together and then points at Matthew.

I roll my eyes.

"Are you really okay?" Matthew asks again, ignoring Mike.

I blush and drop my gaze. "I'm fine."

"Seriously, why don't I get you some ice? I don't want it to turn into a bruise—"

"Hahahaha," Mike chuckles, twirling the ball on his finger, poorly. Doesn't this guy need to get to a bus or something? "I love the idea of you playing nursemaid, Yee. You'd look very cute tending to poor Charlie Dickens who hurt her arm."

I grit my teeth at Mike's mocking tone.

"I'm *fine*," I repeat, throwing my bag over my shoulder. *Ouch.* "Except I need to get home. So move. If we're forced to be partners, let's just talk over text. I can't imagine this holiday concert is all that important to you. I don't even know why you bother with chorus anyway."

Matthew takes a step back, his eyes wide. I feel like a jerk, but now my head is pounding, and my arm is killing me.

I can't get to my locker and out of school fast enough.

Dinner that night is not much better. My parents drop a bombshell.

"Wait, what do you mean you're going to Cleveland?" I cry across the table when they finish telling us about their plans for a mini vacation to accompany Jed's basketball team to the Midwest tournament.

On the first weekend of winter break.

And that Saturday night happens to be the holiday concert. Which my parents definitely knew about (considering I tried to hold rehearsals here and all).

"Well, truthfully, I was hoping we'd all go as a family," Dad explains. "This is a big deal for Jed. If the team wins this, it'll really put them in the spotlight."

The word *spotlight* rankles me. "But what about the holiday concert? This is the year that I could have a solo!"

Or something.

"We didn't do it intentionally," Mom says, and I can tell she's trying to keep her voice even. "We didn't choose the tournament weekend. We wanted to do something fun for everyone. And Cleveland has—"

"Will our hotel have a pool? And a breakfast?" Sadie asks, and I want to glare at her for being a traitor. But I know if I give her one wrong look, I'll be in even more trouble.

I need to focus.

"It's just that Jed has so many tournaments," I argue while Jed silently but happily wolfs down his spaghetti. "There'll be another one in a few months. But this concert is a once-in-a-lifetime opportunity."

Mom doesn't roll her eyes, but she might as well. Instead, she gives me the *try again* look.

"We're always cheering Jed on," I try instead, and I hate

that my voice is cracking, but I feel like the tears are close behind. "I wanted it to be my turn."

"Honey, it's not a question of turns," Dad says. "There'll be other opportunities for you to sing. You have a lovely voice. But if you really don't want to come to Cleveland with us, then I'll ask Grandma and Grandpa to come stay with you. That way they can also make your concert. Would that work?"

The answer is no. The answer is such a strong *heck, no* that I'm afraid if I say it, I'll scream it. But Dad wasn't really asking the question. Because now Sadie is looking up hotels on Mom's phone, and I slink away. This is so typically my family.

"Ugh, I'm sorry," Renee says when I update her that night. I'm hiding in the bathroom, the water running so no one will hear our conversation. Technically, my phone is supposed to be plugged in downstairs right now. But nobody has come to "remind me," so I'm playing dumb about the rule.

If my parents aren't going to support my one major dream in life and attend the holiday concert, I can't be expected to support their rules about screen usage and technology time.

"I don't know why I'm shocked." I stare out the tiny bathroom window. It snowed earlier, but the cold temperature made the snow freeze to ice. While I know it's probably dangerous outside, it makes for a really pretty landscape. "It's so my family to do something like this."

"Well, your grandma is super into Christmas like you, right? So maybe you can use her presence to sneak in an early tree and decorations?" Renee offers.

"Charlie, Sadie needs to brush her teeth!" Mom calls, rattling the handle on the door.

"Can't she do it in your bathroom?" I shout back, ballooning out my mouth to make it sound like I have a mouth full of toothpaste. I'm kind of an expert at this stuff.

"Her toothbrush is in there," Mom reminds me, and I sigh. I'm not as much of an expert as I like to think.

"Did you and Matthew pick the songs for tomorrow yet?" Renee is asking me. "I thought it was smart of Eric to suggest we do that."

I debate pretending I didn't hear her. Is Renee interested in Eric? I don't let the thought settle before I push it away.

"Oops, gotta go," I say, opening the door for my mom. "I'll text you later," I tell my best friend, and hang up.

Sigh.

Back in my room, I open my computer and start playing one of my many Christmas albums (bought with my own allowance because my parents think holiday albums are cheesy). I try to center myself in the voices of Pentatonix.

One day I'll sing in a real a cappella group.

That's the dream, at least.

First step, Christmas concert. Which means, I guess, making nice with Matthew.

I open up my instant chat, find Matthew on there, and send him a message.

Charlie Dickens: So, what are you thinking our song list should be?

The icon beside Matthew's name makes it seem like he's online, but I don't see a response. Maybe he's still at the basketball game. I trail my fingers up and down the computer keyboard.

A-N-S-W-E-R, I tap on the keys without actually typing the letters.

"Charlie, you aren't supposed to be on the computer right now," Dad calls from downstairs. Right. I forgot he and Mom can see me on Gchat, too.

"It's for homework," I yell back, which is mostly true.

Come on, Matthew, I beg silently. I hope he's not mad at me for snapping at him before. I should probably apologize, but . . .

Here's what I'm thinking, I type instead. It's almost easier to write it all down now without Matthew being there on the other end. Let's just pick six songs to start and see how they go. Four that are pretty easy that will allow us to bond as a group. And then two additional songs that will take a longer time to perfect. That way, when we're caroling, we can have four good strong songs, and then two that we're still working on. And then if we decide one isn't working, we can exchange it for another.

It's actually not a bad plan.

"How much longer will you be?" Dad asks from the bottom of the stairs.

Still no answer from Matthew. The whole thing might be irrelevant if he doesn't get back to me.

I consider explaining to Dad how chatting with Matthew—or not chatting, as the case may be—really is homework. Then I decide against it. "Not much longer!" I call back.

"I need to run out to the store and Mom is in her office

working. I want you off the computer when I get back, okay, hon?"

Suddenly, a bubble appears next to Matthew's icon. He's there! He's typing!

"Charlie?" Dad calls. "Did you hear me?"

> **Matthew Yee:** That's a great idea. I think Little Drummer Boy should be one of them because that one is my favorite. ;)

I exhale. He likes the idea. And I can't say no to "The Little Drummer Boy." Though I'm a little surprised that Matthew has a favorite carol.

"Charlotte Dickens!" Dad calls. Eep. When he uses my full name, he means business.

"Yup, Dad, I'll be off soon!" I promise, my heart beating quickly.

"Okay," Dad calls back. Then I hear the front door open and close. Whew.

Matthew is typing again.

Matthew Yee: What about Silent Night as one of our easy ones?

Charlie Dickens: Yes and yes. What about Blue Christmas?

Matthew Yee: YES!

I laugh. Matthew writes in all caps. Who knew?

Charlie Dickens: Tell me you've heard the Elvis Presley and Martina McBride version.

Matthew Yee: Classic! And you and Eric would be great at it.

I blush. It feels a bit odd to talk about singing with Eric . . . with Matthew.

Charlie Dickens: OK, what else.

We end up throwing back and forth tons of song choices, so many that we have a surplus. I'm surprised that Matthew and I are basically in agreement about our favorite songs.

Who'd have guessed?

Chapter Six

"How come you didn't text me last night?" Renee asks the next morning at our lockers.

"Ugh. I wound up Gchatting until late with Matthew, and my dad got mad and made me go to bed."

I roll my eyes for effect. In truth, it was kind of fun to be Gchatting with Matthew. Something about chatting online made him seem less . . . intimidating.

Though it wasn't very fun when my dad caught me still on the computer when he came back from the store. Especially since I was laughing with Matthew about

Christmas videos when Dad walked into my room. After nine thirty.

Oops.

"Did you guys put together the song list?" Renee asks excitedly.

I nod, closing my locker. "We picked three songs that are kind of standards and will probably be pretty easy: 'Silent Night,' 'Santa Claus Is Coming to Town,' and 'We Wish You a Merry Christmas.' And then two songs that will take more work: 'Blue Christmas' and 'The Little Drummer Boy.' We got stuck trying to come up with a sixth alternate, though. There are too many options."

I watch Renee pull her science textbooks out of her locker and hold them as she struggles to shove her coat inside.

"That sounds good," she mutters.

"Oh-kay . . ." Something isn't right. "It's just the list that we came up with. It's no big deal. If there's anything you don't want to do, let's talk about it. Or we can scrap the whole list."

She shuts her locker. "I think we just need different types of songs."

Is she worried I'm trying to steal all the good parts? I cycle through the songs in my head, and I can't figure it out.

"These aren't just songs for me to sing," I tell her. "I think you should take the lead in 'Silent Night' because your voice is great for that one."

"That's not what I'm talking about." At least that's what I think she says. She's walking faster than I am, which means that her words are getting buried in the noise of the crowded corridors.

I grab her sleeve and for a moment she keeps moving, as though she plans to just break out of my grasp. And then she stops.

Thank goodness.

When I take the extra step to reach her, she's staring down.

"I don't know what's going on," she admits. "I know I'm being weird. But I wish all the songs we were doing weren't so Christmas-y."

Of the million possibilities that ran through my head, this wasn't even on the list.

"They're holiday songs," I point out.

"About Christmas."

"Well, yeah," I say, realizing she's right. Despite myself, I bark out an uncomfortable chuckle.

Maybe it was the strangled laugh that breaks the ice, but at least now she's looking at me. "They all feel so religious. And that religion isn't mine."

I lick my lips, trying to figure out what to say. I want to ask what's changed, since last year she didn't feel this way. She watched every Christmas special with me. And she even came to Midnight Mass with me and my grandma because it has the best music.

"For me, the songs aren't about religion," I explain. "They're about great music. And getting to sing on stage. And the magic of the holidays."

Renee nods, softening. "I understand. And I do love all these songs. But . . ."

"Hey!" I have an idea. "Why don't we add a couple of Hanukkah songs to the mix? Like 'Dreidel, Dreidel, Dreidel'?"

Renee brightens. "Or 'Hanukkah, O Hanukkah'?"

I smile back at her. "Perfect."

At lunch, Matthew and Eric come over to sit with me and Renee and we discuss the song choices. The boys are on board with adding a Hanukkah song. We decide to swap out "We Wish You a Merry Christmas" for "Hanukkah, O Hanukkah." The only thing we can't agree on is a sixth alternate song.

We sit in silence, drumming our fingers on the table. Things suddenly feel tense. Then something occurs to me.

"Remember 'Dance of the Sugar Plum Fairy'?" I ask.

Renee snorts. "Who could forget?"

Last year the middle school chorus did an a cappella rendition of "Dance of the Sugar Plum Fairy," which, of course, has no words. All the instruments were replaced by voices, and two of the stars of the football squad dressed up as ballerinas and danced in the middle.

Eric starts trying to mimic the sound, and it's not nearly as good as last year's performance, but then Matthew steps in. And it's dorky and silly and it won't help anything, but then Renee's voice slips between theirs and I jump in, and we're doing a truly terrible reenactment of the performance, right in the cafeteria. Everyone is glancing over at us, but we don't care. It's hilarious.

We hold the last notes a few beats too long, and when I glance around at the group, I'm relieved to find we aren't nearly as stiff and tense as before.

"Okay," I say, clapping my hands. "Renee, what would be your pick for the sixth song? You decide."

"Wait," she says. She snaps her fingers. "What about something fun like 'Let It Go'?"

It's not my favorite song, but it could work.

"Okay with you guys?" I turn to Matthew and Eric, and they both nod.

"I was hoping we could do 'Dance of the Sugar Plum Fairy,'" Matthew says with a fake pout, and it makes us all laugh.

I didn't think Matthew Yee could make me laugh. But I guess he's full of surprises.

The plan is to meet after school at the corner of Maple and Simpson to choose a spot in Lincoln Square.

I'm so excited to go caroling that I'm literally bouncing as I leave my locker. I know it sounds dorky and old-fashioned, but this is the music I love. I love the chimes of bells I can hear keeping time. I love the blending of voices. Carols are the best kind of music: songs you can sing with other people.

And maybe it's that happiness rushing through my body that gives me the hit of courage I need to approach Eric when I see him at the front entrance of school.

"Are you heading to our rehearsal?" I ask.

He's bundled in a hat and scarf and mittens. "I am." He

turns to glance at the door one more time. "Should we wait for Matthew and Renee or will they meet us there?"

Eric is almost a full foot taller than me, and I feel like I need to tilt my head back to talk to him. His big brown eyes are bright.

Forgive me, Renee. "They'll meet us there," I say. And the smile that takes over my face is as close as I can get to laughing without making a sound.

The walk to Maple and Simpson only takes five minutes, but when you are finally walking alone with your crush of the past three years and can't think of a thing to say? It feels like eternity.

"Do you have any plans over winter break?" I ask after we've gone through the boring comments of school, homework load, blah blah blah.

"I'm not sure," Eric says. "My dad recently lost his job, so I think we might just stay home. Not that we usually do anything big, but I think we're trying to do things that don't cost much."

"That sucks," I say. I don't know much about Eric's family, but I remember going to a birthday party in a fairly large house. I wonder if he's worried that he'll have to move.

"It's okay. There are lots of people going through the same thing, especially in my dad's field, which is finance. My brother is taking it harder because he really wanted to go to hockey camp over break and that's not happening now. But he'll get over it. And, hopefully, next year he'll be able to go."

"I'm really sorry," I say. "When did this happen?"

"At the beginning of the summer."

Oh. That's like, six months ago. "I hope your dad finds a job soon."

"Thanks." He smiles.

And while the conversation feels like a real conversation, it also doesn't. I've known Eric for years and yet I didn't know about his dad. And even now when he's sharing with me, the conversation is stilted. If it wasn't for the fact that we are walking, I think we'd both be falling asleep. Like, even standing up.

Two more blocks.

"So are you excited for the concert?" I know I'm scraping the bottom of the barrel, but help me out here, Eric.

"Sure. And it would be cool if our group got the spotlight."

Long pause.

Extra-long pause.

If I fell down, would that make this less painful? At least it would break up the silence.

"What's your favorite—"

"Can I ask you something—"

We're both talking at once, which is truly laughable since there was so much silence we could have been filling. It's like when my mom gets mad when Jed, Sadie, and I fight over the same spot on the couch, as though we didn't have two other couches, plus multiple other places we can hang out.

"Sorry, you go first." There's a little laugh embedded in Eric's comment.

"Sure?"

"Sure."

"It wasn't really anything. I just wanted to know if you had a favorite carol."

Eric exhales, and for a moment I wonder if he thought I was asking a different question. Maybe something more personal? Should I have been? My mind is going a mile a minute and I almost miss what he's saying.

"I guess 'Frosty the Snowman' is fun. You know, standard."

"Oh, good one," I lie.

"There they are!" Eric says, pointing at Matthew and Renee on the corner.

"Wait," I say, stopping him with my outstretched arm. "What were you going to ask? When I interrupted you. And then you said I should go first. But you didn't . . ."

"It was nothing." He shakes his head, his eyes on Matthew and Renee. They are laughing and hopping up and down. It's going to be killer cold to stand outside. I really should have brought warmer clothes. Once again, I chose my outfit based on my bag: brown leather boots, pleated skirt, and fuzzy sweater. But it's my comfort clothing, and I really wanted to feel good today.

"Are you sure?" I ask. What if he wanted to ask me . . .

I can't even think it.

What if he wanted to ask me out on a date?

My heart races.

"I'm sure." Eric's long strides eat up the pavement between us and them, and the conversation is dropped.

It's cold.

Really cold.

Like we probably shouldn't be out here.

We sing through "Silent Night," but it's hard to keep my voice even when I'm trying desperately not to shiver. When people walk by, they barely slow down. We're lucky if they smile. I can't blame them. If I had somewhere warmer to be, I'd be in a rush to get there, too.

"Let's save that one for warmer days," Renee says. "I feel like it just makes me colder."

"'Let It Go'?" Eric asks.

"Are you suggesting a song or telling me what to do?" Renee snorts, and then we're all laughing. And I don't understand why I can't be relaxed like Renee. Eric and I walked all that way and I didn't say anything funny, anything . . . anything. *What's your favorite carol?* I want to facepalm.

"Let's do it!" Matthew says, resuming his jumps. "Come on!"

So we do. And there's something funny about singing the song on such a cold day. We move around as we sing, and start cracking up. Maybe it's the laughter, but more people stop and watch us. An older man starts to join in, his rich baritone a fantastic complement to Matthew's.

"Can we do that again?" I ask when we reach the last note. And there's no disagreement. We run through it another time, and then move on to "Hanukkah, O Hanukkah," because it's also fast-paced. And then we sing "Blue Christmas," twice.

But when we stop, it's colder than ever.

"I can't feel my toes," Renee says, and while I'm pretty sure that mine are moving as I wiggle them, I'm not positive. They feel like thick pieces of ice in my socks.

"How about we take a break and head into the Donut Hole for some hot chocolate and snacks?" Matthew suggests.

"Oh god, yes," I groan.

"I'm in!" Renee chirps.

"Um . . ." Eric hesitates. "I probably can't stay out much longer."

I remember what Eric said, about his family trying to save money now that his dad is out of work. I assume he wouldn't want Matthew and Renee necessarily knowing about this.

"Actually," I say, fake yawning. "I'm suddenly really tired. Maybe we should just wrap up now."

"Okay," Matthew says with a shrug. And I glance at Eric, who smiles at me. I hope he knows his secret is safe with me.

*　　*　　*

"What was that about?" Renee asks. "You weren't really tired."

Renee had texted her mom, who showed up in her car and insisted on driving us all home.

Renee waited until Matthew and Eric had both been dropped off before asking the question, which is good, but I still don't know how to answer. I don't want to break Eric's confidence.

"Is this about Eric's dad still being out of a job?" Renee asks.

"How did you know that?" I snap, and I hate that I feel jealous.

"Eric told me. But he said his dad has an interview next week, so that's good."

After so long feeling cold, my body is overheating now. I shouldn't be getting jealous. I mean, it's no big deal that Renee knows Eric's secret. Or that he told her more than me.

I flick off my mittens and hat, unzip my jacket, but nothing is making it better. I hate the feeling of overheating. I know it's dumb, that it's not like it's life-threatening or anything. But for some reason, it makes it hard for me to breathe, like my clothing is shrinking.

It makes my head hurt.

I can't help looking longingly out the window.

"Mom, do you have a water bottle for Charlie? She's overheating and getting cranky."

I can't believe I snapped at Renee, my best friend who knows me so well. "Sorry," I whisper to Renee as her mom passes back a water bottle and a couple of bags of mini pretzels.

I gulp down the cool water and relax, leaning back. "Thanks, Mrs. Levine," I say.

We drive on for a few more minutes. Mrs. Levine is listening to a podcast series that I know keeps her totally absorbed.

"I don't think he likes me," I whisper to Renee, closing my eyes.

"Who?" Renee asks, but I don't bother answering. It's obvious. Why would I even care if Matthew Yee didn't like me?

"Maybe he doesn't know you well enough," Renee suggests gently. "All we need is Operation Get to Know Charlie, and I'm sure . . ."

She continues talking about this master plan, but I stop paying attention. I feel so dumb because I've been talking about my crush on him forever. But now I don't feel excited about the idea of Operation Make Eric Like Me.

But why? Is that because maybe . . .

I don't really like Eric as much as I thought I did?

Chapter Seven

That weekend, between rehearsals in Lincoln Square, I focus on a new project: Operation Save Christmas in the Dickens House. It's much better than Operation Make Eric Like Me.

When I announce my plan to my parents, they sigh. They insist that we still have lots of time to prepare for Christmas. But I already have a full calendar of events planned.

I've even made a list. And decorated the list, of course.

* Create family Advent calendar

* Set up fancy hot chocolate bar

* Buy a tree, and trim it

* Decorate the house (front and interior)

* Bake Christmas cookies

* Make presents and wrap them!

I stare at the list for several long minutes as I try to figure out which project to take on first. I know I need to hold off on decorating the house, and my parents will say it's too early to get the tree. Christmas cookies should probably wait as well since, knowing my mom, it'll be a one-time thing and I want them around on Christmas itself. Same with the hot chocolate display. And presents? Well, first I need a plan for that.

So creating the Advent calendar it is.

I've never made an Advent calendar before. But I know I can repurpose the trifold I used for my science project. I head up to my room and start to decorate it with silver and red wrapping paper. I sing along to the PTX Christmas album as I work.

It's a good day.

Especially when "The Little Drummer Boy" comes on.

"*Come, they told me, pa-rum-pum-pum-pum,*" I start, pausing in my wrapping job to close my eyes and feel the music.

"What are you doing?"

Sadie's voice might have been quiet, but in my mind I was in the video, singing with Pentatonix. It was quiet there, peaceful, as though nothing could pull me away. Until Sadie's voice.

"Sadie! I told you to knock!" My heart is racing and there's nothing quiet or peaceful now. I feel torn between two different places as the song continues on without me, as though the singers didn't even know I'd left.

Which clearly, they didn't. But still.

"I did knock," she pouts. "But you were singing so loudly, you didn't hear me."

Advent calendar. PTX. Wrapping paper. Happy place.

I need to get back to my happy place.

"I'm making a special surprise for the family." I try to force a smile as I put myself between Sadie and my project.

"What is it?" she demands, craning her neck.

"It wouldn't be a surprise if I told you."

"Can I help you make your surprise?"

My instinct is to say no, to tell her that this is my thing, but maybe that isn't the right idea. Maybe if my parents see how excited Sadie is about Christmas, too, they'll have to get into it.

"I'm making a special Advent calendar for our family," I say, my voice dipping into a conspiratorial whisper. I pull the giant, slightly garish trifold into the space in front of us, and her eyes widen.

"What's that?"

I take out the packets of envelopes I've already started creating. "An Advent calendar is a countdown to Christmas," I explain, placing the numbered envelopes in order across the paper. "You see them sometimes in stores. They usually have chocolates in them and every time you end a day, you get a little chocolate."

Sadie's eyes widen farther than should be possible. "Chocolates every day?" she whispers.

I laugh, but then tighten my lips when her face crumples. Sadie hates it when she thinks people are laughing at her.

"I wish we could have chocolates every day," I say, "but Mom and Dad would never go for it. So instead, I'm putting secret messages in each of the envelopes for everyone in our family. It's not as yummy as chocolates but, hopefully, it will build the Christmas cheer."

Sadie is clearly not as excited as when chocolates were a possibility. Still, her lips curve upward. "Can I help?"

I have to remember, it's the thought that counts, not the way the Advent calendar actually turns out. Though it's turning out cute. It wouldn't go on a Pinterest Fail page.

While I'd collected enough envelopes to fit the trifold so there was an envelope to open every day, it was Sadie's idea to write the numbers in silver (though I nixed the idea of silver glitter because I'd never hear the end of that from Mom).

So it looks . . . fine. A good first try.

"What are we going to put inside all the envelopes?" Sadie asks.

"Messages for everyone. Why don't you help me come up with what to say for Mom, Dad, and Jed's, and then I'll do yours."

"What about yours?"

I shrug. "It's kind of hard to write my own."

I grab the different colored papers—green for Mom's notes, red for Dad's, yellow for Sadie's, and orange for Jed's. I've already precut them, so I have the right amount.

"Huh," Sadie says, and then gets distracted coming up with cute things to write on everyone's slip. "We should do funny jokes for Dad, since his are always so bad. And knock-knock jokes for Jed, since he hates them."

I glance over at her, lifting my eyebrows, and we burst out laughing.

Except, it *is* really hard to think about messages for everyone. Or even messages that can work for multiple people. I throw in a few *Smile!* notes and a couple of *Thanks for being you* before I start to lose my drive. I had this whole plan that it would be some beautiful display and each morning at breakfast, everyone would take a note and we'd all read them out loud just like fortune cookies. And it would make people happy. But I don't know what to say. And frankly, I'm not sure I'd argue with Mom if she thought this wrapping-paper-covered monstrosity should not be displayed in public. It seemed like such a good idea when I came up with it.

I abandon it under my desk. It doesn't need to be the whole month of December, I reason. It will be better if it isn't so cramped with envelopes anyway.

Just as I'm about to open my Pinterest board of possible DIY Christmas gifts, my phone buzzes with a text from Renee.

Renee: Forgot to tell you that Mom decided to throw a Hanukkah party and I know you love latkes.

My mouth waters at the word. As much as I love Christmas, when it comes to food, it has nothing on the culinary yumminess that is Hanukkah. Fried potato pancakes, donuts, and chocolate? It's basically all my favorite foods in one holiday.

> **Me:** Lucky!! Will you bring some to school tomorrow or are you going to eat them all?

> **Renee:** Any chance you want to come over tonight? They will be freshly made.

> **Me:** Yum. Yes. Yum.

> **Renee:** I was actually thinking that maybe it would be fun if Matthew and Eric came, too.

There's a faint uneasiness that swirls in my belly. But I can't back out now.

> **Me:** Sounds great! What time?

When I arrive at Renee's, the Hanukkah party is in full swing. Matthew and Eric are standing in the dining room, rocking the uncomfortable *How did I get here?* look. But

Renee's family is having a wonderful time. Especially her grandpa, who is in his element in the kitchen.

"There's my girl!" he says, giving me a one-armed hug as he flips fried potato goodness with the other hand.

"Mmm," I say, breathing in the smell.

He smiles. "Everyone was poo-pooing my idea of making curry sweet potato latkes, but I knew you'd be in, Charlie!"

Grandpa Leo looks a bit like Santa Claus, minus the red suit. He's round, with a big white beard and metal glasses. But he wears a knit skullcap on his head, the only person I've ever seen wearing one in real life. But, then, there's the suspenders he always sports that tip him back to Santa category. And the way he laughs. Exactly Santa.

"What other kinds have you made?" I ask, trying to peer past his roundness into the galley kitchen.

"No peeking," he says, turning to block the counter. "We're doing a taste test, just like always."

I used to feel bad for Renee that she doesn't celebrate Christmas. But that was before I witnessed what went into their Hanukkah celebration. Renee's family doesn't do a Hanukkah bush, or other Christmas-like things. Instead, their traditions are all their own. Grandpa Leo's family came from Syria, so when he's in charge, the food he creates smells and tastes completely unlike anything I'm used to. Grandma Anna's family, on the other hand, came from Russia, where latkes are made from onions, potatoes, and oil. Every year, part of the Levine family tradition is the taste test Grandpa Leo referred to. But it's not just latke versus latke. They go all out, creating special sauces and dips, and there's enough food to last the entire holiday.

I explain the story of the dueling culinary traditions to Matthew and Eric as we help set the table. Just as always, Renee's mom has taken out all their family's Hanukkah menorahs, everything from the ones that Renee made in preschool out of clay and sparkly paint, to a cool new one made of shiny glass. For each of the eight nights of Hanukkah, Renee and her mom light their own candelabra, but when guests visit, there are always enough for each of us to get our own Hanukkah menorah. It's kind of like a modern day Hanukkah miracle.

"Holy fire hazard," Eric mumbles, and I laugh.

"I remember once I was here on the last night, and the only time the candles were left unattended was for five minutes. We all traipsed outside to see the candles lit from that angle. It was beautiful."

There's a lull in the conversation as I get lost in the memory, and not for the first time, I wish my family had the love of tradition that Renee's had . . . even if it's a totally different tradition.

"Are we ready to light?" Grandma Anna asks. She hands out cards with transliterated Hebrew words. She lights the candles, and recites the blessing, and we all sing along where we can, even Matthew and Eric. Then the four of us break into a rendition of "Hanukkah, O Hanukkah." It's fun.

"Now let's get the table ready for the contest," Grandpa Leo exclaims. "I don't want Anna to claim she didn't win because hers got overcooked."

He winks across the room at me, and I laugh. He always makes the same statement, and the best latke award always goes to Anna. I'm not sure what she puts in hers, but she's able to pull ahead no matter what spices he puts in his. I think it might be because Grandpa Leo votes for hers instead of his own.

"If I don't like mine, can I give them to you?" Eric whispers to me as we're given a sample of each latke.

"You'll like them," I whisper back. My stomach flips at how close we are to each other.

"I need a backup plan just in case," he insists. Our faces are so near, it's almost like we're breathing the same air, except I'm not really sure I'm breathing at all. If it weren't for the fact that we're sitting at Renee's dining room table and her whole family is around us, I'd wonder if maybe he was going to kiss me. Except . . . we are at Renee's dining room table with her whole family in the middle of Hanukkah dinner, and Eric is eating his latke and exclaiming how much he likes it. And everyone is talking and there's music playing and I'm just . . . in shock?

I go through the motions of eating and smiling and writing down a vote, but inside, my brain is swirling around and around.

Does Eric want to kiss me?

"So which did you vote for?" Grandpa Leo interrupts my reverie.

"I—" I startle.

"Oh, come on, you know she voted for mine," Grandma Anna says. "Now teach these boys how to play dreidel. They've never played! Can you believe it?"

*　　*　　*

That night, I call Renee just as I'm supposed to be going to bed.

"Tonight was super fun," I whisper. "It was exactly what a holiday dinner should be like."

There's a long pause, and Renee yawns. "You know you can come over any night of Hanukkah, right?"

"I know." I remember watching Eric and Matthew playing dreidel, how Matthew won (of course), and the look of pure joy on his face. "I just wish my family were more into Christmas."

There's a long pause, and I curl up tighter on my bed. It hasn't even snowed again, so outside it just looks cold, no snow to soften the outdoors.

"Is it bad that I like Christmas so much?" I ask, my voice so quiet that I almost wonder what I spoke and what I thought.

"Of course not," Renee says. "I think it's just hard to understand for some people," Renee continues as if I hadn't spoken. "Like, is it because of your name, or do you really feel that way?"

"Hey!" I straighten my body. "You know it's not because of my name."

"*I'm* not saying it is," she hurries to add. "Eric asked me that and I told him it wasn't. But I'm just saying—"

"Eric thinks I'm obsessed with Christmas because of my name?" All my anger morphs into sadness.

"We were just talking about it. He didn't think that's why you like Christmas. He just asked the question."

I don't know if I'm more upset that Eric thinks I like Christmas because of my name or that he and Renee were talking about it. It makes me wonder when he said that: If it was before we whispered together at the table or after? And if it was before, did it mean he changed his mind about me? Or if it was after . . .

Or maybe there was nothing to our heads drifting so close.

"Okay." I know I should finish the conversation

properly, that Renee is going to be worried, but I can't deal with anything more. "I've got to go. I'll see you tomorrow morning?"

"Are you mad at me?" she asks before I have a chance to disconnect. I debate hanging up anyway, pretending I didn't hear her, but that's not fair.

"I'm not mad," I answer truthfully. "I'm just tired and a little sad." And then I do hang up the phone, because I don't have anything more to say.

Chapter Eight

Luckily, everything feels back to normal the next day. And soon, the four of us fall into a rhythm of practicing. We bundle up and gather in the park to sing again on Monday and Tuesday afternoon. And so long as I don't overthink any interactions that Renee and Eric have, I'm okay.

The best part is that we're actually starting to sound good. People now stop to listen to us, and some even ask us what days we'll be downtown and come back to hear us again.

Which is kind of crazy. But also really amazing.

Singing outside has also helped us find a theme for our spotlight rehearsal. We've become The Carolers, and for some reason, the group listened to my suggestion that we should all stand in a line, hands clasped in front of our stomachs as we sing. I only wish I'd taken my grandma up on her offer to teach me to knit last Christmas. Then I could've knit us matching scarves so we'd look even more professional. And maybe I could have even made us one of those old-fashioned white muffs to keep our hands warm. Though the boys may have protested that.

On Wednesday, we're just about at our regular caroling spot when Renee sees the lights.

"Charlie! Look!" Her shout is jarring enough to get my attention, but the addition of the sharp poke in my side? I stop abruptly.

"What?" I have perfected the ability to not get sucked into Renee's excitement before I know what is fueling it. It could be that there's a giant concert in the middle of downtown, or a real live movie star walking in front of us. Or a three-legged dog. Renee has two settings: excited and not excited. There's no gradation.

"The lights. On the rink. They're on!"

My breath hitches. That *is* excitement-worthy. The outdoor rink in the park was supposed to have opened already, but it kept getting delayed. But the lights on means . . .

"There are people skating!" Renee squeals.

Renee loves to ice skate. She even used to skate competitively, when she was younger. I love it, too.

Eric and Matthew finally realize that we aren't behind them, and they backtrack to where we're standing. If my expression is anything like Renee's, we look like two puppies at a window.

"We should head to practice," I say reluctantly. We do need to really be on top of our game.

"We've practiced all week. Maybe we could skate first and then practice?" Renee suggests. She hasn't moved her gaze from the skaters, and I find myself being pulled along.

I'm even wearing what would be a cute skating outfit: my brown wool pleated skirt with matching tights, an oversize navy knit sweater that used to belong to my dad when he was in college, and a matching scarf and hat set. And while so much of that is hidden beneath my long coat, if we were skating, I'd get warm and then I'd probably be able to take off the coat and . . .

"I have to get home by five, so I don't think I could do both," Matthew says. "But if you want to skate instead of caroling, I'm down with that. We've been doing a lot of singing, and it wouldn't be bad to have a break."

Matthew stares at Renee, and not for the first time, I wonder if she has an admirer. That would be a huge coup to have a guy like Matthew Yee interested in her. It's sad to say, but at our school, just the interest of a popular guy—or girl—makes a difference.

And maybe then I wouldn't feel so bad whenever I see her and Eric together.

I shift my gaze to Eric. I don't need a popular guy to be

interested in me. I've always been interested in Eric. He may not be a sports star like Matthew, but I've liked him even before he shot up in height, back when he was just skinny and short.

"I'm fine either way." Eric smiles, being agreeable just like always. "It's up to you guys."

"Please, please, please," Renee begs, her hands clasped in prayer. "It'll be so fun and I don't think most people even know that it's open, so it's pretty empty."

Maybe Matthew will want to skate with Renee, and then Eric and I can skate together. Maybe we'll even hold hands, and it'll start to snow and . . .

I know that conversations are happening around me, but I don't tune in until I hear my name.

"Sorry, what?"

"I said we should do it." Matthew shrugs. "But it's been a long time since I've been on skates. For the sake of the school basketball team, any chance you'll help me out, Charlie?"

I'm grinning so hard at the possibility of being on ice that I don't realize he's asking me and not Renee, until I'm already nodding my head.

"Wait, Renee is actually a much better skater—" I begin, but Renee and Eric are already halfway across the street. I glance at Matthew and he gives me a winning smile.

"Please?" he asks.

"Fine," I say with a sigh. "But you better not drag me down."

Since it's opening day, the ice rink is loaning out skates for free and the ice is fresh and clean. Like Renee predicted, it's also pretty empty. That and they're playing Christmas music, which is totally perfect. Especially since Matthew doesn't seem to mind that I'm singing along. At full voice.

It takes a few times around the rink before I'm in the skating groove and feel ready to dump my coat on a bench.

For all Matthew's warnings, he's actually not a bad skater, just rusty. At first I try to give him pointers, but given his quick progress, I'm able to focus on how great it feels to be on skates.

I know that most people hate winter, and that my cousins in Arizona don't understand how we can live in this cold weather. But I wouldn't give it up for anything. I can't imagine Christmas without the lights twinkling against the bright snow, or the trees with their very real icicles. Sledding, skating, and downhill skiing are my favorite forms of exercise, and while I've never tried snowshoeing or cross-country skiing, I'm sure I'd like them, too.

Also, if I lived in a place without winter, I'd miss my beloved cold-weather clothes. Like turtlenecks and thick sweaters, tights and tall boots. And mittens. I have an unhealthy obsession with mittens.

"What are you thinking about?" Matthew asks. We've gotten into an easy rhythm of skating side by side, our strides just about in sync, and I'm positive that my face has the same glow that his does.

"Just how much I love this weather," I say. "And how I want to take my grandma up on her promise to teach me to knit over Christmas. Apparently I buy too many mittens."

Matthew's smile is wide, and it doesn't even bother me that up ahead, Renee is holding Eric's hand as he wobbles on his skates. Because I'm getting to skate quickly right now, and as much as I'd love to hold hands with Eric, this is a fabulous substitute. There's cool wind and warm muscles, and my cute skating outfit is, in fact, the perfect skating outfit.

"So is the whole Dickens family as caught up in the Christmas spirit as you?" Matthew asks.

I falter as I glance up at his face to see if he's making fun of me. But Matthew's eyes convey interest, not mocking.

"My grandmother has always really been into Christmas.

But I think my mom had overload growing up, so she's not as much of a fan." I focus on my strokes, right, left, right, left, and Matthew stays quiet.

"Is this the same grandmother who's going to teach you to knit?" he asks, and I look up in surprise. Sure, it wasn't that long ago when I told him about it, but I didn't really expect he was paying that much attention. I mean, we were just making conversation.

I nod.

"Sounds like you guys have a really special relationship. Just like Renee and her grandparents," he says quietly. "I'm kind of envious." His voice is soft, and I'm surprised he admitted that.

"I feel lucky," I admit. "Even though I don't get to see her that often. She lives in Maine. But when she and my grandfather come to our house for Christmas, she and I make dozens and dozens of Christmas cookies. And she sneaks some decorations around the house, so it doesn't have to be just in my room."

The noise of the other skaters fades away as I think about how much I look forward to her visit.

"My dad's parents died when I was little," Matthew says. "And my mom's parents live here, but they're in a retirement community. They used to have this awesome house with a lake out back. And I'd sleep over when I was a kid, and my grandfather and I would go on these long walks and he could tell me about every different kind of bird we'd see. But now . . ."

There's a pause, and I wish I knew what to say. I can't imagine my grandparents having to leave their big house in Maine. My dad sometimes laughs that my grandfather won't leave until he's carried out on a stretcher, but suddenly that doesn't feel as funny as it usually does.

"They just have a one-bedroom apartment at Auburn, and while it's really nice and they've made it their own, it's not the home that I remember." Matthew pauses again, this time just briefly. "Sorry if that sounds dumb."

"It doesn't."

We've stopped on the side of the rink, and I'm facing him. I never thought I'd be having such a long conversation with Matthew Yee, never mind having him share all this stuff about his family.

"Can I ask you something?" I blurt. "Why are you in the chorus? You have so many things you're already a part of; it's not like you need more things to do."

Before Matthew can answer, we hear shouts and screams from across the ice.

"Oh my god," Matthew says. I whip around and see him racing to the center of the rink, where both Eric and Renee are now flat on the ice.

"Help!" Eric yells, and that's when I realize the screams are coming from Renee.

By the time I get to Renee, Matthew's jacket is around her shoulders. There are two boys standing by who look like they're probably in fourth grade or so, and seem vaguely terrified.

"Are you okay? What happened?" I ask when I'm able to get through the crowd that has now gathered around them.

"It wasn't my fault," one of the kids says, and he shoves his friend, hard.

"Stop it," orders Matthew.

"They bumped into us," Eric explains.

Renee's sitting up, but one leg is lying on the ice at an odd angle, and she's sniffling.

"We should take off her skate," Eric suggests, but Matthew shakes his head.

"Let's carry her off the ice so she can warm up a bit. Sitting on the ice can't be good for her."

"Let me." A guy who works at the rink is pushing toward Renee, but there's no way he's out of high school, and he's sliding all over the ice. I shift my eyes along the crowd until I see a man who looks like a dad.

"Can you please help us?" I ask, and he's picking Renee up off the ice before Skates Guy is even there. Everything is moving so fast, and yet so slowly. Renee weeps. By the time we have her settled on the bench with my long coat now covering her, we hear the wail of the ambulance.

"Can you call my mom?" Renee stutters, and I nod quickly as the EMTs do some preliminary checks of her body. By this time, both of the boys responsible appear scared out of their minds, and one looks like he's going to cry.

"I'm so sorry," one of the boys whispers, his face just as white as Renee's. "I just haven't been on skates for a long time and I wanted to go fast and I didn't see you. . ."

"Just be careful next time. You really could have hurt someone," Eric says, his words gentler than I would have expected. But that's not what really gets me. While Renee isn't crying anymore, her face is void of all color and I'm glad she's sitting down because otherwise I'd worry she was going to faint. And Eric is sitting by her side, his arm around her, and she's leaning into him.

I know it's dumb, and I know Renee is hurt, but the combination of fear and anger and cold do ugly things to the inside of my body. I want to lash out. I want to displace Eric, shove Matthew in there instead. If he'd been skating with her, none of this would have happened.

"He did hurt someone," I snap. "If you hadn't been so careless, Renee wouldn't be lying here . . ." *with Eric*, I want to add. Somehow I manage to push those words down into my belly. But there's more that has to come out.

"Charlie, it was an accident." Matthew's voice comes from far away, and I can't focus on it. Because right now Renee's mittens are off and she's holding on to Eric's hands tightly, and I can see the concern on his face, and I hate how awful it makes me feel. If only Renee had been paying better attention to her surroundings. If she'd been skating with Matthew, she would have been okay. But no, she had to skate with Eric, even though she knew that I liked him. And now—

"It might have been an accident," I growl, "but that accident has messed up everything. How are we going to rehearse for the showcase spot if Renee has a broken leg? And if she drops out, we won't have a soprano. And . . ."

I know that the words coming out of my mouth are awful, but I don't know how to stop them. All I can see is Renee and Eric, her head on his shoulder, her hands in his.

And she's crying now. "Is that really what you're thinking about right now?" Renee sobs. "The concert? You don't care that my leg is hurting so much, and I'm going to the hospital and it might be . . ."

She's full-on sobbing now and the guilt is so thick inside me that it feels like it's replaced the blood rushing through my body. My limbs feel cold and sluggish and the reality of what I just said comes down full force.

"I'm . . ." I start, my eyes filling now.

"Come on," Matthew says, his words gentler than I deserve. "Let's let them get Renee in the ambulance right now. And isn't that her mom over there?"

His tone soothes me, which succeeds only in making me feel worse about myself. I can't believe I said all those things. But now Renee's mom is here and she's a tornado of movement as she rushes to her crying daughter.

I take advantage of all the activity to slip away unnoticed. I trade my skates back for my boots and walk home, my watery eyes blurring my vision.

What have I done?

Chapter Nine

I spend the next day in bed. I tell my mom I'm sick, and for once, she believes me. But the truth is, I can't deal with going to school. Renee hates me. I acted horribly, and in front of Eric and Matthew, no less. And there's no chance we'll get the showcase without Renee.

Last night, when I got home, I started working on the "I'm sick" story so my family wouldn't bother me. And today, when Mom comes knocking at the door, I pretend to be sleeping. Deep breath in, deep breath out. I throw in a hitch just for good measure. I hear a tray being lowered about fifteen seconds after the smell of tomato soup fills my room. Tomato soup and a grilled cheese sandwich, if I'm not mistaken.

It's hard to remember to keep pretending to be asleep when my stomach wants to pole-vault right out of my body and attack the food beside me.

I have a zero percent chance of surviving a Zombie apocalypse, a fact that is only made more clear when my stomach groans in protest when I don't jump on the food.

I hold my breath, expecting that any minute now, Mom's going to sit beside me on the bed, one hand on my forehead, smooth my hair back, and want to talk about why I've permanently banished myself to my room.

Except she doesn't. She does the hand on the forehead, the sweeping back of hair, but she doesn't take a seat. Maybe I'm a better faker than I'd thought?

"I talked to Renee's mom. Unfortunately, it looks like Renee broke her leg. She's home now but she's apparently really exhausted, so Elyse said it would be better to wait to visit," she whispers. "And by the way, the grilled cheese will taste better if you eat it while it's still hot." And with that, she shuts the door gently behind her.

I let out the breath in a rush. And then pull myself up, grabbing one of the sandwich halves and my phone. Who cares about faking, or losing in the Zombie apocalypse—my mom's grilled cheese is delicious. Though, before I allow myself a bite, I type out a text to Renee.

> **Me:** I'm the evil troll who took over Charlie's body. I'm so sorry about your leg.

Renee sends me back a thumbs-up emoji but nothing else. I'm really going to need to make this better.

I stay in my room for the rest of the afternoon, even when Sadie and Jed come home from school. I hear hushed voices from outside, Sadie whining, the hint of Mom's calming voice. Jed dribbles his basketball for a while, and then when Mom yells up the stairs, he quickly shoves everything in his bag and races downstairs. I'm so used to his noises, I don't even need to see everything to know. And then I count to four, until Jed races back up the stairs, and there's the tossing around of stuff in his room until he finds what he's looking for. My guess? His phone or his sports glasses. Right now he's relaxed, but I know the next time he races up the stairs—from the car this time—he's going to be in a bad mood.

I don't get why he can't remember his stuff the first time. Especially since I can apparently predict with startling accuracy what he's missing.

Boys.

Thinking about boys reminds me of the way Eric looked at me after I finished ranting.

I can't believe I said all those things.

I can't believe that Renee and I fought. That thought has me diving back under the covers for another pity party. Jed might not be able to remember his basketball equipment for his daily practices, but at least he didn't yell at his best friend like a lunatic.

*   *   *

The house has been peaceful for an hour when there's a knock at my door. I debate pretending to be asleep again, but the door opens before I have a chance, and Dad peeks his head in.

"You have a visitor downstairs," he says, with the hint of a wink.

Or maybe he has developed a tic?

But either way, my heart leaps. Because that means Renee is willing to talk to me, which means that maybe I didn't utterly destroy our friendship.

"It's a boy," Dad adds, and my heart drops.

Except . . .

"Wait, are you sure?"

My dad chuckles. "Unless you know girls named Matthew? I mean, I might be wrong. Maybe I should go ask him—"

"No, no!" I jump out of bed, my feet tangling in the covers, which almost results in a graceful face-plant.

Agh. What is Matthew doing here? Is he going to yell at me for how I treated Renee? Or . . .

No. He must be here to yell at me.

"But listen," Dad is saying, "I have to go run some errands. Is it okay if I leave Sadie with you?"

"Uh . . ." My head is still reeling from the knowledge that Matthew is downstairs right now. What is he doing here? "Of course," I manage.

"Maybe just get out of your pj's before you go downstairs." Dad winks again. "It could only help."

Pj's are likely the least of my problems. I don't even want to look in the mirror for fear that it will be clear I'm already part of the Zombie apocalypse.

You're beautiful just the way you are, Mom would say if she was here.

A swipe of lip gloss and everything looks happier, Grandma would say.

You could have an hour and you'd still look like a troll, Jed would say.

And Sadie . . .

I can hear her little voice with her tiny lisp that grows more pronounced when she's around my friends who think she's adorable. Shoot. Sadie must be down there with Matthew. And that propels me right out of the room. After a quick change of clothing, that is.

Sure enough, Sadie is sitting beside a very amused-looking Matthew. She's telling him the story of how she's about 75 percent sure that the tooth fairy isn't real, but that she goes along with it for Mom and Dad.

Sure she does.

It isn't until I step on the last stair—the one that squeaks—that Matthew turns and sees me. The smile he gives me is wide and real, and maybe it's possible he didn't come to yell at me for my atrocious behavior?

"Oh, you're finally out of our room," Sadie huffs, her advanced theatrics in full gear. Even though she's only seven, she clearly has a bright future ahead of her in acting. "Mom said I couldn't bother you while you were pouting—"

"I wasn't pouting. I didn't feel well."

"Right." She gives me a look that I know she learned from one of those TV shows I wish they'd take off the air. The ones with the sassy children and the bumbling adults that make me want to deprogram Sadie every night.

Though truth be told, I'd totally be on Team Sadie when the Zombie apocalypse comes. She'd have them all believing we were already zombies.

"Why don't you go upstairs now? Since you've been wanting to for so long." I try to keep my tone light and happy, but there's an edge to it, one that I'm sure Sadie can hear.

"She's adorable," Matthew says as Sadie huffs up the stairs.

"She's something," I mutter as I flop down on the chair across from the couch where Matthew is sitting.

I want to do this right, but I don't have the faintest idea what one is supposed to do when a boy comes over. If Mom was here, I think she'd offer him cookies?

"Do you want—" I start, but evidently the urge to fill the silence isn't mine alone.

"I hope it's okay—" he says, and then we both laugh.

"You go first," we both say, and then repeat the awkward chuckle. Only, because it's Matthew, it's actually not really that awkward. He motions toward me to go ahead, and I smile.

"Do you want a snack or a drink or something?"

He glances around uncertainly and maybe I did that all wrong, maybe I was supposed to offer him something different? I'm about to backtrack when he nods slowly.

"Sure. I actually didn't have lunch today, so I'm kind of starving if you have something. But if you don't . . ."

"Come on," I say, motioning to the kitchen with my head. "I make a mean grilled cheese sandwich if you like those. And I'm sure we have some more tomato soup."

"Sounds perfect," Matthew says, and from that moment on, through the making of the grilled cheese sandwiches and the heating up of the soup, the conversation is no longer stilted in any way. We don't talk about chorus, we don't talk about carols and showcases, or Renee and Eric. We don't even talk about why he's at my house. Instead, he asks about Sadie and tells me about the testing he had done when he was her age, and then offers to talk with her about it or try to help her out.

Everything in my life feels mixed up. I've hurt my best friend and lost my chance with the boy I've liked forever. And yet the boy I thought was a jerk is actually . . . kind of nice to hang out with.

Until we start talking about my family's attitude about Christmas, and then it goes from kind of nice to epically hilarious in a matter of minutes.

I hadn't been intending to talk about Christmas. In fact, if you'd asked me earlier in Matthew's visit, I would have paid money not to talk about it at all, for it to be January and for Christmas to be far behind me. But then Matthew asked me about our lack of Christmas decorations and everything kind of came out, including how my parents were planning a trip over the weekend of the concert.

"Wait," Matthew says, his face so serious that I grow worried. "Your family doesn't make you pose for Christmas pictures? Your parents' friends don't still talk about the picture of you when you had no front teeth and how cute you looked? Your dad doesn't have all the old cards framed on his bookcase at work? What kind of parents are they?"

He stares at me with such fake pity that I can't stop the bubbles of laughter that burst out, even with my hands plastered over my mouth. Though that was mainly to keep myself from snarfing out my orange juice. The good news is I was successful at least in that.

"We only once posed for a family Christmas picture," I say, swallowing, "and that was because my parents thought it would be hilarious to make an ironic version of the traditional card, with all of us wearing ugly Christmas sweaters."

"Tell me you still have it." Matthew's eyes widen, and he scans the kitchen we'd just tidied up as though the photo might be hidden somewhere here.

I begin shaking my head, and he raises his eyebrows.

"You totally still have it."

"Nope," I laugh, and I can't remember the last time I felt this loose and happy around a boy. I guess maybe Matthew isn't so bad. He is kind of fun to be around. "Or at least I don't have a physical copy of it anymore."

He starts moving toward the kitchen door, and I grab his arm. And then let go, because is that okay? To grab his arm like that?

But Matthew doesn't seem to think it's strange. Instead, he takes advantage of my dropping his arm to take my hand, and he pulls me into the living room. "Show me where you keep the picture," he orders, using what I could only assume is his best fake TV villain accent.

"Never," I whisper.

He narrows his eyes. "Maybe I'll just have to ask Sadie," he threatens, and the laughter that I'd only barely contained before comes leaping back out.

"No! No! Leave her out of this."

Our voices must be louder than I'd thought, because a door opens from upstairs. "Charlie?" Sadie calls.

Matthew looks at me sternly. "Tell her it's all fine," he whispers into my ear. "You don't want to get your sister involved, do you? Because who knows what other pictures we might find if I ask her for embarrassing photos of you."

I can't help it—I shiver. Because while I know he's being silly, while I know it's just a game, I love this moment. I know that if I tell him to stop, that I don't want to show him the picture, he'll back off. But there's something exciting about this game. And I don't want it to end. It's like a private little joke between the two of us.

"We're okay!" I call up to Sadie, and her door closes again. "I'll take you to the picture," I tell Matthew, trying to appear defeated. "Just don't get my family involved."

Which is how we wind up at the computer in the den, sitting side by side. After I show him the picture, and he has a good laugh, I make him pull up the Christmas pictures of him and his parents that his mom has uploaded to their family website, on a page that has more Christmas bling than we've had in all the years combined.

The room has darkened around us and I'm barely aware of the time passing. This feels surprisingly natural. And fun.

Then we start searching for Christmas music videos. It starts with Matthew being shocked and appalled that I'd never seen the Hallelujah Chorus flash mob.

"Oh my god," he mutters, grabbing the keyboard out from under my fingers. "You cannot live another moment without watching this video. How someone who loves Christmas and Christmas music so much hasn't watched a Hallelujah Chorus flash-mob video is beyond me. It's practically a crime."

He's staring at the computer screen as he talks, which gives me the opportunity to focus on him. He's pressing his lips together, a move that I recognized from school as what he does when he's really excited to say something, like he has to physically keep his mouth closed for fear that it will come out on its own. Like when he knows the answer to the question that the teacher has asked someone who doesn't know it, and he so desperately wants to get them off the hook. I used to think he was full of himself, like he needed to prove to everyone how much smarter he is than everyone else. But I realize that's not it at all.

"You're a good guy, Matthew Yee," I say quietly, and at first I don't think he hears me because he doesn't stop typing. And maybe that's okay. Maybe that's better, in fact, because I probably shouldn't have said that out loud.

But he turns to me and even though the only light in the room comes from the computer screen, I can tell that he's pleased. "I always thought you didn't like me," he admits, and his honesty surprises me. His honesty and the hint of sadness in his voice.

I shake my head, trying to find the right words. "I don't think I really knew you at all."

He shrugs. His head begins to turn back toward the screen, but I will it not to—I will him not to end this conversation because I don't know what's going on here, but I don't want this to be the end.

Miraculously, his chin reverses course and his eyes find mine again. He stares at me for a long minute, and then he smiles. "I think you're a really good person, too, Charlie Dickens."

Which is when I remember Renee and what I said to her, the look in her eyes and in Eric's. "A good person wouldn't have said those awful things yesterday," I blurt.

And just like that, all the sadness gathers back in the pit of my stomach, and my eyes fill.

Please let it be too dark for him to see that I'm about to cry, I beg the universe.

"Good people sometimes say the wrong things," Matthew says.

"Why are you being nice to me?" I ask, my honesty a surprise. Usually I'm much better at protecting myself, pretending I don't care, but I can't seem to do that right now.

"Because I know all about saying the wrong thing and reacting badly," Matthew says quietly. "And I know this isn't who you are, it's just something that you did. And there's a big difference between the two."

I want to hold his words in my hand, cup them gently and examine them. I need time to figure out if they're true.

Except at that moment, a key turns in the lock in our front door, and in pour Mom and Dad and Jed. For a second, I want us to hide, I want to continue the pretense that it's just Matthew and me alone, that we're in this protected bubble, the outside world blocked out.

But before I even have a chance to formulate a plan, the light in the den flicks on, and all three of them are staring at us in confusion.

"What are you guys doing sitting alone in the dark?" Mom growls.

Chapter Ten

In the end, it's okay. Mom believes us when we say that we didn't realize how dark it had become as we sat at the computer looking for Christmas music. And before I know it, Matthew is fist-bumping a very stinky and sweaty Jed, who apparently won the game for his team.

Mom and Dad invite Matthew to stay for dinner, and after a quick call to his dad, he accepts, but nothing is like it had been before. Apart from the three minutes Jed takes for a shower, Matthew stays glued to him from the minute he walked through the door, grilling him about the game and the training camps he's attended. And Jed is eating it up.

And I'm . . .

I feel like I lost something I only just got, and part of me doesn't know for sure what it was, because it all happened so quickly. I want Renee to still be my friend so I can excuse myself to go to the bathroom and call her and dissect the entire conversation with her. I want . . .

I want to go back in time before everyone walked in. Before basketball-great Jed arrived home. Before Sadie came bounding down the stairs, batting her eyelashes at Matthew.

Before I returned to my place as the forgotten child.

Dinner is all basketball talk at first. Then Sadie actually listens to Matthew talk about the learning issues that he dealt with as a kid, and how much having techniques to work through them has helped him. And I know I should be happy, and I am. But meanwhile, the meal feels endless. It's made so much worse because Matthew is sitting right beside me, almost as close as we were by the computer, but that *feeling* of closeness has disappeared. It makes me reconsider what happened.

Maybe Matthew just came over to talk sports with Jed, since he'll be trying out for the high school basketball team.

I'm standing to clear the table when I hear my name mentioned. I'm so lost in my own world of reasons for Matthew coming over that have nothing to do with me that I don't hear the context—only that it was a question someone asked Matthew about me.

Please don't let it be embarrassing. Please don't let it be embarrassing.

"Charlie said she'd never heard 'Feed the World,' and I thought that was so sad for someone who loves Christmas music as much as she does." Matthew turns to me after addressing my dad, and the smile is the same one he'd given me earlier, open and light and all for me.

My mom stares at me as if she's never seen me before. "Of course Charlie has heard 'Feed the World,'" she insists. "Remember, it's the one from the eighties with all the British singers?" She turns to my dad. "How did it go again?"

"It's Christmas time," Dad starts, his voice deep and rusty. But under his beard and mustache, the smile peeking through is undeniable.

"And then something about not being afraid." Mom hums a bit and then Dad joins in, and between the two of them, they basically rattle off the entire song. Or at least I think it's the song.

I turn to Matthew, who nods. "Your parents know it," he whispers, and I'm not sure if he's trying to be funny or not, but the admiration in his voice makes me giggle.

"Was that really it?" I ask. Mom and Dad are laughing about something and Sadie is begging them to sing it again and Jed is smiling and suddenly the world's worst dinner just reversed itself.

Especially when Mom turns to Matthew and asks, "Did you say you've seen the music video? It's still online? I vaguely remember watching it when I was your age—"

"Probably over and over, knowing you," Dad interrupts.

"Okay, fine, over and over," Mom concurs, pretending to be annoyed. "But the singers were super cute. And they seemed like real people and . . ."

"They weren't cute," Dad scoffed. "Except for—"

"I could pull it up on the computer," Matthew says, his voice cautious, as though he's afraid of startling a wild animal. Given that I'm frozen in place, I definitely understand his concern.

And then suddenly we're all in the den, crowded around the computer screen, Matthew in the middle as though he's the only one who knows the secret code to finding this video on the Internet. Except, it's kind of fun—the excitement, that is. And the fact that everyone is in on it, that

Jed's not on his phone, that Sadie isn't watching TV, that we're all together.

It only gets more fun when we watch the video, which has terrible quality and the least attractive musicians of all time. Until you look at Mom and Dad's faces and see how they are transformed watching it. They have their arms around each other, singing along, and even Jed doesn't have a quip to make about it.

Jed leaves when we start talking about watching it again, but he's back right away with a printout of the lyrics for each of us in time for the chorus. Matthew reaches over and restarts the song, and maybe it *is* the Zombie apocalypse, because I can't believe what's happening.

Suddenly we're that kind of family. The family I've always dreamed of. The ones who gather around the piano (okay, fine, a computer) and sing Christmas songs (even cheesy songs from the eighties). After we've exhausted that song, we start pulling up other Christmas songs, ones with karaoke-style lyrics at the bottom. Some are funny while others are sweet, but all that matters is that we're all in this together.

It's like my family found Christmas again, and all because of Matthew Yee.

I really need to talk to Renee.

Chapter Eleven

On Friday morning, I stake out a spot in front of Renee's locker a good fifteen minutes before she usually gets to school. I thought about calling to apologize last night, but I wanted to do it in person. After four years of never fighting, I need to do this right. I had a whole speech prepared, which all dissolves in the air when I spot her walking down the hallway, talking with Eric. Eric, who is holding her bag on one shoulder and her coat on the opposite arm.

She's so focused on her conversation with him that I don't think she sees me until she's almost right in front of her locker. At first she smiles, like this is any other day, not the day after one and a half days of not talking. And then her mouth pinches, and she twists to look at Eric.

Eric is holding her stuff. Did he just see her at the front entrance and offer to help, or did they arrange to meet?

My stomach clenches and for a moment I can't breathe.

"Hey, Charlie," Eric says and deposits Renee's bag beside me. He glances over at Renee and then places her coat on top of her bag. "Do you want me to stick around and . . ."

Renee shakes her head, though her eyes are still on me. I can't quite figure out what's happening, whether she's still mad, whether I'm now mad. Is she interested in Eric? Do I still have a crush on Eric? Does he like Renee?

Eric walks off and Renee and I stand facing each other.

"Um, I kind of need to get in there," Renee says, her voice quiet. Her head is tilted down and I follow her gaze to her cast.

"Sorry," I mutter. "Nice cast." The bright blue plaster covers her leg past the edge of her skirt, and I wondered if it stops there or if goes all the way up. Man, it would suck if it was a full leg cast. How would she take showers? Or exercise?

"Thanks." She struggles at her locker, trying to put both crutches under one arm and balance that way, but the ground is slippery and it's hard to get traction.

"Can I help?" I ask, and then take the question out of her hands by turning the lock myself. It's a good thing that best friends know each other's combinations.

Are we still best friends?

"I'm really sorry about Wednesday," I say, my words falling over themselves in the rush to get out. "I shouldn't have said all those things. I know you didn't go out to steal Eric on purpose . . ."

"How could you even think that?" Renee's voice was buried in her locker, with me on the other side. "You can't steal a person. And I'm not interested in Eric. I like him a lot, it's true. I never realized what a nice guy he is. But even if you weren't interested in him, I wouldn't be. I'm not interested in anyone. I'm not like you. I'm not thinking about boys twenty-four-seven."

Her words sting but I deserve them. And if that's what she needs to say to even things out, that's fine, too.

There's a long list of questions I wish I could ask. *Are you still going to stay in our group?* That one is at the top, followed by: *Can you still be in the concert? Why aren't you interested in Eric? Do you think he's interested in you? What if I'm now interested in someone else?*

Things were so much easier before middle school. Crushes were things whispered between friends, not lived out in real time. They were like happy little secrets that lived in our hearts and slipped away when we got bored with them.

"I need to get to class," Renee says quietly. Only then she notices that her coat is still on the floor. Her shoulders slump forward, and I know that defeated pose. It's what she used to look like at her skating competitions when she'd given it her all but she knew it wasn't enough to win.

"I'm sorry," I whisper, and I take charge. I may be the worst with words, but I can make things better with my actions. "Just move over a bit and I'll get everything put together."

"You don't have to," she says, but her words are rough with the tears that are on their way.

"I do," I say, not looking her in the eye. Instead, I reopen her locker and put away her jacket and then take the books she was trying to figure out how to carry along with her backpack while on crutches. "Come on, you're going to be late for English and you know how Mr. Gerstein gets angry when he has to restart the attendance record."

I start walking and hope she's going to follow.

"Your class is in the opposite direction," she says from behind me. "*You'll* be late."

"I know, but I deserve to be yelled at. And since you aren't going to be the one to do it, I'll just have to take it from Mrs. Shaw."

Renee doesn't respond, but I can hear her crutches behind me.

I have so many things to fix, but first on the list is Renee. Then I can deal with the question of Eric. And maybe even the question of Matthew.

Sometimes I feel like I'd do anything to be back in elementary school. Even if it meant missing out on the concert.

For the rest of the morning, I carry Renee's books from class to class. I tell my teachers that I was assigned as her helper, which gets me out of my classes a few minutes earlier to get Renee to her classes. I didn't tell them that it was self-assigned, but whatever. I have bigger problems.

Namely: Renee is still not talking to me. I respect it, and I won't push her if she's not ready, but it's killing me. And there's only so much small talk I can make without bringing up our fight, the concert, or Eric and Matthew. There just isn't that much going on in my life beyond that.

Finally, at lunch, I take action. Instead of carrying Renee's tray and bag to our usual table by the windows, I keep walking until we're all the way in the far corner of the room.

Most kids don't like to sit here because it's a little dark and gloomy, but I need dark and gloomy right now. Or rather, I need cover.

"Um . . ." Renee looks around nervously when she finally catches up to me. "This is ominous."

I wish her words held humor but they don't. They're almost frustrated.

"I wanted to be able to talk." I don't make eye contact, but instead slide her food off the tray, setting it up the way she likes it, like it's a real meal at a café instead of a fast-food joint. Those are her words, not mine. I'm perfectly fine with this being a fast-food joint.

"Given how long it takes me to walk anywhere," Renee says, carefully easing herself down onto the chair, "it's either eating or talking, and for once, I choose eating."

"Then you eat and I'll talk," I say, plopping down beside her.

"But—"

"Eat," I demand, and she does.

I grab a few fries and shove them into my mouth for inspiration. The truth is, I have no idea how to make this better.

"I wanted to say I'm sorry," I start. "I was awful on Wednesday. I wish I could explain it, but I can't. It's like some crazy monster took over all my thoughts and feelings and kept winding them tighter and tighter inside me."

She raises her eyebrows, and I shrug. "Yup, that sounds even crazier. I guess so much feels like it's been building up to this concert, but now nothing is working out. My parents have to choose that one weekend to go away, and the concert almost gets canceled, and I thought that Eric would finally see me for once, and nothing . . ."

I lose steam, unable to meet Renee's gaze. Because I still haven't said what I need to say. "But none of that is really important," I admit, finally lifting my head. "When you got hurt, I was terrified. And not for the concert, but because I was scared for you. It's just that instead of saying *that*, all this other junk came streaming out. And I'm so, so sorry."

Around us, people are packing up their lunches. Part of me wants to grab a few more fries, but another part of me is too nervous to eat.

What if Renee doesn't forgive me? What if she forgives me but doesn't want to be my best friend anymore?

What would I do without Renee?

"It's okay," she says quietly. "I was scared, too. Everything was happening at once, and I guess I just needed you to let me be the scared one while you were the brave one. And instead—"

"I was the crazy one and Eric was the brave one."

She stares at me for a long moment before she nods. "I meant what I said before, though. I'm not trying to take Eric away from you. Or take his attention away. Or—"

"I know." Suddenly famished, I stuff another handful of fries in my mouth. "I'm a total dolt." Those words are muffled by all the fries in my mouth. We only have a few minutes left, and while eating is still really key, so is finishing what I have to say. "You're my best friend. *That's* the most important thing."

She smiles, the first time it's reached her eyes today.

"Well, that and getting the showcase," she teases.

I stick my tongue out at her.

"Kidding. Kidding," she laughs.

But I wonder: Is it bad that I really *do* still want to win the showcase?

After school, the four of us carolers meet in the library.

"So, bad news and good news," Eric starts once I've put Renee's stuff on the table and she's hopped over on her crutches.

I don't dare hope that the good news will cancel out the bad news.

"Now that we can't carol on the street, we're kind of stuck," Matthew starts. "We thought about trying to convince our parents that we should rehearse at home, but that didn't seem like a great idea. Plus, I think it's been really working for us to have an audience." Even though this is so far all bad news, Matthew is still smiling, which is . . . odd.

Unless he doesn't want to do the concert? I wonder what he thinks about last night. Whether it seemed dorky to him once he got home and talked with his real friends, or if he actually had as much fun as I did. "So I talked to my grandparents. They live in an assisted-living facility downtown called Auburn. I told them about how it's going to be difficult for Renee to stand and sing for caroling, particularly in the cold, and they said they're always looking for folks to come and sing there."

He glances over at Eric, who nods.

"They also said . . ." He stumbles over his words, which is odd because Matthew never misspeaks. But suddenly it seems he doesn't know where to look. "They said that they'd like us to stick to more of the old-fashioned songs. Like more of the Bing Crosby kind of hits rather than the modern stuff."

I stare at the tabletop. Books and planners lie scattered in the middle, and I'm afraid to look up. Afraid to look at Eric (Is he mad?), afraid to look at Matthew (Does he think I'm weird?), and afraid to look at Renee (Is she going to go for this?). What if Renee doesn't want to do any of this anymore? What if—

"It doesn't really change our song list that much, but maybe we could shift our theme a bit. I don't know what to really call it, but after talking with my grandparents, I started thinking about what our audience would want to hear, not just what we want to sing. And"—Matthew glances over at me, his rich brown eyes holding mine—"maybe our theme could be an old-fashioned holiday? Like more of the songs that used to be on the radio, the ones that bring back memories."

I shift my eyes to Renee, who seems just as surprised as I am. She opens and closes her mouth a few times before giving a nervous giggle. "I think it's a great idea. I could talk to my grandparents about what songs they remember."

"Does that mean you're in?" Matthew smiles, and suddenly I feel ashamed of how I misjudged Matthew in the past.

Renee nods. "I have to ask my mom of course, since now it'll be harder for me to take the bus places."

"Charlie?" Everyone is staring at me and it feels a little awkward. Okay, it feels really awkward. On the one hand, I'm so relieved that we're still a group. But on the other hand, is this going to be enough to win us the showcase?

"Sounds great," I say, trying for excitement.

"Great!" Eric's voice is just as fake chipper. "They said we could go tomorrow, and I know Matthew has a basketball game but that's in the early afternoon. If everyone can do around 5 p.m., I think it could work."

We all nod—awkward, awkward, awkward—and then stare at the middle of the table.

"So, should we try to make a new list?" I ask, and everyone groans, but I already have my phone out. "Here's what I'm thinking . . ."

We spend an hour poring over a song list, trying to keep as many of the songs we'd practiced as possible, but throwing in some new ones, too. Now we'll just have to wait until tomorrow to see how it all works out.

Chapter Twelve

Saturday afternoon, my dad insists on driving me to Auburn Senior Living Estates to make sure the building's management is really okay with us singing there. I'm not sure what kind of ruse Dad thought we were pulling: Were we trying to foist holiday songs on a bunch of unsuspecting seniors?

Except, as much as I should be thinking about our song list and whether we're prepared for this concert, all I can think about is watching videos with Matthew and how much fun it was.

"We're here," Dad says, opening the door. I startle out of

my reverie to notice that we've already parked and he's turned the car off.

I need to get my head in the game.

The Auburn Senior Living Estates is an odd name, because there are no estates here. It's a collection of low buildings. Any thoughts I had about an expansive property with trees covered with snow and Christmas lights come to a screeching halt as I see the parking lot. And the grocery store. Though there is a cute little stationery store that I'm going to need to check out one day.

"This is so interesting," Dad says as we enter the building. "I've always wanted to come inside and I've never done it. But it makes so much sense."

"It's an apartment building," I remind him. "I'm not sure what's so shocking."

"No." Dad shakes his head, turning to glance around the building's lobby. "A library, brilliant."

The thing about Dad is that he's obsessed with urban planning. Every time we drive to a new city, we get the rundown on how the city was built, what mistakes were made, what challenges they faced. When we took a trip to Boston last summer, Dad made us all go on an extensive city tour. Which, apart from a few cool facts, was epically boring.

In Dad's dream, one of us studies urban planning in college, mostly so he can live vicariously through us. Because as much as he loves to learn about it, he isn't changing careers from being an accountant. Mom has made that very clear: He can buy as many audio courses and books as he wants, but until it's time to retire, he isn't leaving his job. Just like Mom isn't going to stop being an optometrist just because she's obsessed with marine life.

So while I'm vaguely interested in what might be fascinating Dad, I'm a little worried it'll just lead into some boring lecture about architecture.

"This building is what's called a NORC. It's a naturally occurring retirement community," Dad explains excitedly. "The folks who've lived here have been here for decades, and as they got older, the city decided that it made much more sense to bring services into the building rather than have all these people needing to leave their homes. So there was the grocery store we saw. Inside here, there's a small post office, a library, and a medical facility. And they plan social events, too, so that the adults here don't wind up stuck inside their apartments. It's really genius, but there aren't many places where they've popped up. I should talk with Matthew's grandparents about their experience here. I'm sure they were involved as the building changed over."

I make a quick scan around the lobby. I shrug. "It looks like a regular old folks' home."

Dad turns to face me, his eyebrows pulling together. "This isn't really an old folks' home, Charlie. Many people raised their children in this building, and thanks to donors and the city, they're able to stay in their homes instead of being moved to a new place, which might be nice, but has none of the familiarity of home."

Thankfully, I spot Renee coming through the doors, so I'm able to escape my dad and his ode to all things city planning.

Things still feel spotty with her, so I don't give her a hug but offer to take her bag instead.

"I'm fine," she says.

"I've got it," her mom says, coming up behind her.

"Mom, I'm fine." Usually, Renee and her mom are so close, they're almost like a mother-daughter pair on TV. But something is not right at the moment. And to add to it, I can tell that her mom is definitely not happy with me.

"I know you're fine," Mrs. Levine tells Renee in a fake whisper. "But the doctor said to be careful. And I don't want you to injure something else."

Renee's jaw clenches. I get it; her mom didn't want her coming to rehearse. Now I'm grateful that my dad is coming toward *us*.

"Hi, Elyse," he says to Renee's mom. "Renee, I heard about your fall. I'm so sorry."

"I'm fine," Renee says again, looking down. She's shifting her head back and forth in tiny movements, which I recognize as the first sign that her hair is bothering her.

"I'm planning on staying here and speaking to some folks about this building," Dad says, still caught in the glory of the NORC. "You're welcome to hang out with me if you'll be waiting, Elyse. There's some fascinating things. Or I could just bring Renee home after the kids are done singing."

Elyse blanches and her eyes dart to Renee's head. "If you're sure you're okay here, hon," she says, "it would probably be helpful if I went grocery shopping and picked up the dry cleaning. But that's only if you're okay getting a ride back with Charlie and her dad."

"Perfect." The sharpness in Renee's one-word answer makes it clear that she's moments away from losing it. So before she has a chance to say a word, I grab her bag from the floor and start walking along the foyer.

"Come on, this is a great spot to wait for Matthew and Eric," I say. I dip into the front pocket of her bag and pull out an elastic.

"Thank you," Renee mutters as she takes a seat beside me. She slouches off her coat and it's only then I notice the faint sheen of perspiration on her face. "Do you think your dad did that on purpose because he knew I was moments from killing my mom?"

I glance up at my dad, who is coming toward us. He winks at me and gives me a quick half smile. He totally knew. Oh, Dad. When we get home, I'm definitely asking him more about NORCs and what he discovered.

It's surprisingly easy to get set up once Matthew and Eric arrive. Mr. Carlson, a friend of Matthew's grandparents, meets us in the atrium, and it's funny to watch how serious we all get, shaking hands, thanking him for the opportunity. My dad and Eric's dad both stay with us while Matthew's mom visits her parents upstairs.

"So how should we do this?" I whisper to Matthew.

"Oh, we have it all arranged," Mr. Carlson says as he points us to the other side of the atrium. There are at least two dozen people sitting in chairs arranged in a semicircle around an open space.

"Are they here for us?" I whisper, but no one answers. I think we're all stunned into silence.

"We don't really need a stage area," Renee says. "It's not really a performance. Before I hurt myself, we were just standing downtown and caroling and people could walk by and—" She takes a sharp breath in. "And, you know . . . leave."

"It's just that we don't have that many songs," Eric is quick to add. "We kind of depend on people only staying for a little bit and then moving on."

I want to join in, but I'm entirely focused on how sweaty my palms have become.

"They'll leave when they're ready," Mr. Carlson says, moving us along to our performance space. "They're not expecting a show. But we don't tend to create events where people have to stand. It's just not fair to most of them."

I immediately feel guilty that I'd wanted them moving and walking. Of course they don't have the same mobility as the shoppers on Simpson.

Matthew and I hang back as the rest of the group moves forward. "What are we going to do?" I mutter, and he shakes his head slightly. "We only have six songs that we've practiced, and one of them is from *Frozen*."

"Keep singing the same songs over and over again?"

We're now steps away from the rest of the group, and my stomach is doing something that reminds me of those old movies with planes flying in circles. The atrium is big and filled with light, and I'm not entirely sure how our voices will sound in this cavernous room. But it'll be good practice. That is, if they don't get totally bored by us within a few minutes.

Mr. Carlson introduces us, and that only makes me more nervous. He makes us sound professional, like an actual group.

What if the audience feels like this is a waste of time?

I glance over at my dad and he gives me an encouraging smile.

For a long moment, us four carolers all kind of stand in the middle of the open space, unsure what to do.

"Do you guys sing? Because I can't hear anything but I'm not sure if it's just my hearing aid." The woman who's talking appears older than most in the room, though not because of the color of her hair. Which is blue. Not like a bluish tint. Like almost exactly the color that I've wanted to put in my hair since last year. My mom insists I have to wait until high school.

"Um, yes." I'm choking on the words, but at least I'm

164

speaking. Apparently, the rest of the group is struck dumb. "The thing is, we aren't really a *group* group."

"Speak up, I can't hear you." This time it's a bald man at the other side of the cluster of people.

"Um . . ." I say to him. My mom hates it when I say *um*, but in this case it's the only word I can get out.

Disaster. This is going to be a disaster. I turn to my dad, but he's deep in conversation with Mr. Carlson and another man, one who looks awfully like an older Matthew from a distance.

"Oh, Hank, don't be ridiculous," the blue-haired woman says to the bald man. "You know perfectly well that you can hear just fine. You just wanted that pretty girl to talk to you!"

The rest of the crowd chuckles, but it's not the awkward laughter of a situation that's getting out of hand. It's the sound of a group of people who are really close. The blue-haired woman stands up, using the back of the seat in front of her for help. Holding on to the shoulders and hands of her friends, she takes the ten or so steps necessary to get to where we're standing. She glances up at me, and her smile is pure radiance.

"Don't you let us intimidate you. We're just having some fun because we get bored easily. We know you aren't a real group, that you're practicing for your holiday concert. We're just here because we love music."

"Speak for yourself," Hank calls out. Looks like she was right, he can hear perfectly well. "I'm here because they promised cookies."

"Come on, then." The woman takes my hand, and it's only then I notice that she's swaying slightly. Her grip is firm and cool on mine. "Let's do some caroling. Do you have a repertoire or do you just wing it?"

I'm staring in disbelief at this tiny woman with bright blue hair, holding my hand. But then Matthew comes up from behind me and joins in our little line.

"Hi, Francine," he says, moving to take her other hand.

"Matthew, don't you flirt with me. There are girls here who are far more appropriate for you." Francine gives me a wink and I can't help but blush.

The crowd chuckles, and then before we know it, Eric has brought a chair for Renee, and our little quartet has become a quintet with Francine in the middle.

"Can we start with 'Silent Night'?" Francine looks up at Matthew, who glances at me, and I can see Renee and Eric nodding as well. "It was my George's favorite." Her voice shakes a little, and I feel an odd pulling sensation from inside my chest, like suddenly my heart is too big for my body.

Matthew counts us in, and Renee takes the lead. Her voice is rusty at the beginning, but I can feel it fill out as Matthew joins her, and then Eric and then me. We're singing it the way we practiced in school, and while there are some missteps—like the fact that apparently Francine can't remember all the words—there's something special about the way it sounds in this room, with this group.

When our voices die down, we immediately jump into "Let It Go," as though we're singing on the street again. If this had been a performance, we would have allowed for a few moments in between the quiet stillness of "Silent Night" and the exuberant "Let It Go." But after our experience caroling, we know it's best not to let the crowd mourn the end of one song, not to let them think too much.

But also, it's for us as much as them. There's a sadness to "Silent Night" that makes it a hard act to follow. But somehow the simplicity and pure happiness of "Let It Go" is the perfect antidote, and I feel the crowd with us as we sing. Several of the people in the front row are tapping their feet, their hands gently clapping. And of course Francine remains front and center between us, as though she is as much a part of our group as any of us.

From there, we move into "Hanukkah, O Hanukkah," and then Eric and I step up and we launch into "Blue Christmas." And even though things are still odd and strained from last week, there's a lightness when we sing this together. There's something that feels very alive as we join our voices together in the song.

Just before we're about to end the set, Matthew steps forward.

"This is one of our favorite carols," he announces to the audience. "And I think you'll all be wowed by Charlie and her amazing rendition of 'The Little Drummer Boy.'"

My stomach gives a small flip. I smile gratefully, not sure how to understand that introduction. But instead of dwelling on it, I take an extra moment to center myself, to get into a space where I can lead the song.

This is my song.

I close my eyes and take a deep breath.

"*Come, they told me,*" I start. And just like every time, I'm amazed by the sound that Matthew, Eric, and Renee make when they sing "*pa-rum-pum-pum-pum.*" The music fills all the spaces around me, loosening my body, relaxing me.

"*A newborn king to see . . .*"

"*Pa-rum-pum-pum-pum,*" they sing.

I'm not even pausing; the timing is perfect. It's as though they have their music and I have mine, and I've gone on to "*our finest gifts we bring*" in time for them to start up their *pa-rum-pum-pum-pum* again. It feels so much better to sing this song in the warmth of the atrium rather than the cold outside. And even though I know we're not on stage and this isn't a concert, I can't help but feel the moment of perfection. We head into the last *pa-rum-pum-pum-pum* and I end with "*me and my drum*."

There's silence, a great big giant moment of silence. And before I'm even aware of what I'm doing, I turn to Matthew.

His smile is wide and happy, and nothing else really matters.

I'm faintly aware that the audience has burst into applause.

"That was beautiful, dear," Francine says, and she takes my other hand so that now she can squeeze both hands. "My mother used to sing just like that. My George used to like it sung faster, but I've always been partial to the slower version."

I don't know if it's her age, or if she's remembering her mom or her George, but her eyes are bright and watery. And maybe it's contagious, but mine are now watering, too. Our audience is slowly filing out, and Renee, Eric, and Matthew are accepting their thanks.

I can't move. I want to bring Francine home, bring her to my mom so she can tell her what she told me. It's the song that brought back the memories. This simple song that took her back to listening to her mom sing it and to maybe arguing with her husband about the tempo.

That's the power of songs. They're traditions. More memory keepers than a collection of notes and words.

"Thank you," I whisper to Francine. Her smile has none of the strength of Matthew's, but it's somehow more powerful.

Hank comes over to our makeshift stage area and offers Francine his arm. "You still sing beautifully," he tells her and I don't know if I just didn't notice her rouge before, but her cheeks are a deep pink now. "Are you ready for dinner?"

Francine pulls me close, and I bend my knees slightly so I don't tower over her. "Thank you for letting an old lady have some fun," she tells me. "Now I'm off to a dinner date." And she winks at me again, and maybe this isn't intentional at all, maybe it's nothing really, but she shifts her gaze from me to Matthew.

Did she see me smile at him?

It's only later that night, much later, in my bed when I'm trying to fall asleep, when I ask myself the question that has been brewing in the back of my mind.

Why did I look at Matthew?

Chapter Thirteen

I can't wait to go back to Auburn to sing some more.

But Monday brings its own surprise, which I discover when Renee pulls me by the arm down the corridor.

There are many wonderful things about Eleanor Roosevelt Middle School, but natural light is not one of them. Thankfully, the school invested in bright lights to make the hallways seem less dingy. But still, if you asked most kids in the school, they'd admit to walking out of their way in order to pass the huge picture windows at the end of the A wing.

Today, it seems like all those kids not only walked past but couldn't help themselves. They stopped to stare.

Snow. And not just flurries. And not a gray slushy mess.

Pure, white flakes. Snow that sticks.

"Wow," I whisper, my breath creating a fog circle against the windowpane. It took a bit of maneuvering to reach the front of the crowd, but I'm willing to use my elbows in order to see the snow. "How long has this been going on?"

"I think it started just after first bell." Renee's voice is wistful, and I imagine her injury is feeling even worse than before now. No skating on the park rink. No sledding. Not to mention, it'll be even harder to get around on crutches.

Normally, Renee's favorite way to walk on snowy days is to go through the deepest part of the snowdrift. It'll take her four times as long and she'll be exhausted afterward. But she'll be grinning like a madwoman.

The warning bell goes off and if I'm going to make it to my last class on time, I'll have to majorly book it across the building.

"Meet you after school by our lockers?" I ask, and out of the corner of my eye, I see her head bob. It's hard to look anywhere but the glittering white surface covering the field. It's already at least a foot deep, and it's still coming down. I don't know how I missed the forecast for today. Or rather, I do know. I've been pretty focused on rehearsals.

"It's a good thing we moved our caroling to Auburn," I say.

While I've managed to pull myself away from the glass, Renee remains where she is. And I realize that I need to find some way of giving her a snow adventure even with her broken leg.

I slide into my seat just as Mr. Gerstein begins class, and luckily, he's just going over the homework assignment he'd given us last time.

In the corner of my notebook, I doodle a sled and little hills of snow. I can tell that this snowfall is the perfect sledding weather. It'll pack down nicely, and I can already imagine the sensation of whizzing down the hill at Point Pleasant Park.

I draw a string on my imaginary sled and stare at it for a long moment. It might not be safe for Renee to go shooting down the hill at Point Pleasant. But what if we could make a fake sleigh ride for her? She'd be so excited. I could grab the battery-operated twinkling lights and attach them to the big sled we have for when we double up . . .

I'm so deep in the daydreams of sledding that I don't hear Mr. Gerstein's question until he's standing right in front of my desk.

"Charlie? Do I need to speak louder?" He's wearing a smile, but he's not at all amused. The rest of the class, on the other hand . . .

I smile meekly. "Sorry, Mr. Gerstein. It's just the first real snowfall and—"

"We live in a climate that is going to be plagued by snow for the next three months," he growls. "I don't see what the excitement is all about."

Maybe we should take Mr. Gerstein on the fake sleigh ride. The thought of his lanky body folded up on our kiddie sled makes me snort out a laugh. "Sorry," I mutter, flipping my notebook to hide the sketch I made. I keep my head down.

Even though I can't see my English teacher's face, the sigh he lets out speaks volumes.

"Now," he goes on, "I was asking who here had time to read the short story . . ."

I manage to focus and answer Mr. Gerstein's question.

But I don't stop thinking about sledding.

I'm the first one out of class when the final bell rings. This probably doesn't improve Mr. Gerstein's opinion of me, given my earlier behavior. Especially since I've spent the last seven minutes with my filled backpack on my lap.

All I can think is that Matthew would understand.

The hallways start to get crowded as people slowly leave their classrooms, but I'm single-minded in my determination.

I zigzag around kids stopping to chat, and if I could have, I would have leapfrogged over Addison Sinclair, who stopped to tie her shoelace. (I veered around her instead.)

"Hey!" I blurt out when I reach Matthew's locker, panting. He's still fiddling with his lock, so he couldn't have gotten there much before me.

"Hey!"

His smile is wide and genuine, and I wish I could talk right now instead of needing to focus on breathing in and out. I probably should have planned this better.

"Need . . . your . . . help," I gasp.

"You okay?" He leans against his locker, no longer trying to open it. His brows furrow and I realize I must appear to be in bad shape.

"Fine," I nod, trying to seem less desperate to breathe. I really need to go back to swimming or running. Or something. "It's Renee. She loves sledding. With her broken leg, I want to figure out how to give her a sledding experience."

His head bobs up and down, and now that I know Matthew, I know this means he's processing all this information.

"I'm assuming you're thinking we need a sled she can't fall out of, like one of those old-fashioned ones? We can tie a rope through the front and . . ."

Now it's my turn to lean against the locker bay, because when Matthew gets excited about something, it's fun to just step back and get out of the way.

By the time we meet Renee at my locker, my cheeks hurt from smiling so hard, and both Matthew and I are waving our arms excitedly.

"Wait, I can't understand either of you! One at a time," Renee demands.

I turn to Matthew and he to me. And looking at his flushed face, I know that his excitement mirrors my own. Two weeks ago, I couldn't have imagined that Matthew and I would be able to get through a rehearsal together. And now it's almost like we're . . . friends? I stand back to let him explain our idea. And it's totally awesome.

Except Renee says no to our convoluted plan to get her on a sled. Apparently, she doesn't want to take the risk of injuring herself again, which totally makes sense. Except, I really wanted to go sledding.

"Just because I don't want to go barreling down the hill with an already broken leg doesn't mean I don't want to come along to watch," she says, her words tumbling over themselves as she catches sight of my disappointed look.

By now, Eric has joined us at the lockers.

"Why don't we sit on the bench," Eric says to her. "I'm personally not one for barreling down a hill, broken leg or not. But I'll keep you company?"

I wait for the normal jealousy to rush in, but . . . it doesn't. Instead, I laugh.

"Why are they making it seem like sledding isn't the most fun thing ever?" I ask Matthew in an overexaggerated whisper.

"No idea." He shakes his head and then shrugs. "You going to back down?"

"No way."

Forty-five minutes later, Matthew and I are standing at the top of Magic Mountain, the big hill in the park next to school, with a few dozen other people. Actually, a lot of Matthew's popular friends are here. But he's still standing beside me.

We've chosen a spot on the far side of the hill, because it's close to the path and the park benches, which makes it much easier for Renee to cheer us on. Well, Renee and Eric, that is. I wait to feel a pang when I see them deep in conversation, but I can't find it. I should be upset, but in reality, right now it's hard not to grin.

Especially since Matthew is trash-talking me.

"Listen, if you want me to go slowly because this is your first time out on the snow, I mean . . ."

"Stuff it, Yee," I answer. "I was practically born on a sled."

He wrinkles his forehead.

"Too much?" I grin. "Maybe you should sit this run out if you're feeling queasy."

He winks at me. "Let's do a few practice runs and then we'll see who should take it easy."

I drop down to my sheet of cardboard and I cross my legs in front of me. Then I wrap my scarf around my nose and mouth, securing it under my jacket by rote.

Matthew just ties a solid knot in his scarf, and flings the ends behind him.

"No way, mister," I admonish. "No getting strangled on the first run down."

And then before I know what I'm doing, I'm leaning over to where he's sitting on *his* sheet of cardboard. I balance on one knee on my "sled" and I quickly undo his knot.

"Chin up," I say as I carefully wrap his scarf around the bottoms of his ears and up to cover his mouth and nose. I've done this dozens of times for Sadie, and it's not until I'm tucking the ends deep into the collar of his jacket that

I realize I'm touching Matthew Yee. I'm arranging his scarf. I'm—

Oh. My. Goodness.

"Sorry," I whisper, and drop back to my cardboard. "Um, let's go!" My cry is halfhearted, but my desire to escape from the moment is strong. As a result, I dig my mittens into the soft snow, trying desperately to propel myself down the hill. I know it's not really a fair start, but the mortification keeps me going even as I hear Matthew behind me.

I can't believe I did that.

But I don't have much time to dwell, because the plastic that Matthew insisted we tape onto the bottom of our cardboard is whizzing me down the hill, and it's all I can do to hold on. The crisp air is sharp against my exposed skin, but it feels amazing. I don't know if it's just the air or the fresh snow. Or Matthew. But halfway down the hill, I let go of all my anxiety and start screaming like a banshee.

Why can't I spend my life sledding?

I finally come to a stop about twenty feet beyond the bottom of the hill, and I don't move.

Wow.

"Holy moly, you were fast!" Matthew says, slowing his improvised sled by leaning to the side. He skids to a stop beside me, and his eyes are bright and twinkling. His words are muffled by his scarf (oh my goodness, I did that!) but his glee comes through loud and clear.

"The plastic bottoms worked great," I croak out, and he winks. Matthew Yee winks at me.

"Want to go down again? But this time, let's start at the same time so we can actually race."

I chuckle into my scarf. "It's not going to make much of a difference. You'll still be eating my snow!"

We take six more runs down the hill. Sometimes we decide to judge based on speed, other times on distance. We keep track with a makeshift scoreboard created with twigs. By the sixth time, the snow in our racing track has been beaten down pretty flat, and the sky has darkened around us. Renee and Eric left after run four, and while at first I was going to walk with Renee, in the end, the possibility of continuing the races proved to be too enticing.

"Last run?" Matthew asks. I glance around us. While we aren't the only ones still here, most of the other kids are gone. I shiver. Somewhat from the cold but also from . . . something else. Something that I'm having a hard time naming.

"Winner takes all?" I say, trying to tame my voice.

"Fine. Ready to try going backward yet?"

I shake my head. That's way beyond me. I mean, I'm a hard-core sledder, but backward is terrifying and defeats the purpose. The whole idea is being able to see everything whizz by as you fly ahead. "How about on our stomachs?" I suggest.

My mom would freak out if she saw it, but I did it dozens of times last year, and the conditions are definitely better now than they were then. "We've done this run enough times that we know there's no debris on the snow. And few people here. So . . ."

"That might be too scary for me," Matthew says, but I know he's joking. All this time together and I feel I can read the truth in his eyes. "You may need to hold my hand."

I snort, trying to hide my blush. "That would make it much more dangerous."

"Then what if, instead, we go down together? We can put our two sleds together, you can go in front, and we'll—" His voice drops. "I mean, if you want."

I glance over at the empty park bench where Renee had been sitting. Why couldn't she still be there? I need to talk about this. I need her to see this!

"Okay," I find myself answering. "How do we do it?"

And that's how we wind up at the top of Magic Mountain, our two makeshift sleds connected as best we can. I sit in the front, with my knees up, and Matthew sits directly behind me. We don't really talk as we set ourselves up because, really, this is a crazy idea. These aren't even real sleds.

And now Matthew is going to have to hold on to me by putting his arms around my waist.

I'm finding it hard to breathe. Luckily, my coat is huge and puffy, so I can barely even feel it when his arms circle me.

Otherwise, I wouldn't be able to concentrate at all on the sledding. It's already a big enough problem.

"Are you sure this is okay?" Matthew asks, and it's too hard to dislodge the words from my throat. So I just nod. "Should I push us off?" I nod again.

Matthew drops his arms from my waist, and he digs his hands into the snow. This is our last run, I think. Who knows if Matthew and I will ever go sledding together again? And even if we did, it wouldn't be like this. It wouldn't be just the two of us with the sun setting around us. It wouldn't be fun and easy like it is right now. But before I can feel any more sadness and nostalgia, Matthew has us moving down the hill. As we pick up speed, his hands move from the snow to reband themselves around my middle.

I want to play it cool. I want to seem like this isn't a big deal, but I can't help it because this is totally different from going sledding with my brother or with Sadie. Or even with my cousins over winter break on a real sled. And so instead of crossing my arms around my bent knees, I splay them out to the sides, and I scream.

Which is probably what causes us to go tumbling down the hill.

It happens so quickly, I don't even feel anything before we hit the bottom. One second I feel free and wild, and the next my face is down in a pile of snow and I'm lying on my stomach.

Beside Matthew.

I don't seem to have broken any bones. But I'm worried about Matthew. I turn to him. "Oh my god, are you—"

His eyes are wide. Could he be in shock? Could he—

"I can't believe you toppled us over on the last run!" He sits up and laughs. "Next time you're going to yell like that, warn a guy so he doesn't let go in fright."

I scramble to my knees, the wet snow permeating my jeans. Without thinking, I push his shoulder, toppling him back into the snow.

"Oh, you're going to pay for that," Matthew warns, laughter in his voice as he gets to his feet and starts packing a snowball.

"Mercy! Mercy!" I call, darting away from him. I'm freezing cold and covered head to toe in snow, but I can't remember having been this happy in a long time.

And the memory of Matthew's shocked face when I threw a snowball at him after playing the "mercy!" card keeps me warm through most of the walk home.

As does the memory of his arms around me on the sled.

Chapter Fourteen

After the Day of Awesome Sledding, as I've taken to calling it, us carolers buckle down and Auburn becomes our regular destination after school. Thankfully, Matthew's busy basketball schedule is done, and if anyone in the group has other things they want to be doing, they don't tell me.

We sing and we sing and we sing.

Each time we come to Auburn, there's a different crowd. Sometimes it's twice the size of that first afternoon, often it's less, but each time, Francine and Hank are there.

We call them our regulars.

We have regulars. It makes us laugh.

The only problem is that they aren't interested in hearing the same songs over and over. They all have suggestions and requests. And while in the beginning I try to keep us to only one or two new songs, I quickly discover that if we want our audience, we need to be flexible. So I bring a book of holiday songs and between that and our phones, we wind up being able to find the lyrics and chords for any song that they want, as long as we mostly know how to sing it. Which might be a problem because while our range is increasing, our level of polish is not. I try not to let it get to me.

Francine has taken to bringing sweet treats and setting them up on a table beside the giant Christmas tree and menorah in the lobby. She makes killer chocolate caramel cookies and lemon bars. And these brownie type of things called Nanaimo Bars. She says they're a recipe from growing up in Canada, that they're incredibly easy to make, but I can't imagine that's true. Once she discovers how much I like them, she starts making them all the time.

I should tell her to stop, but I don't. Because they're really, really good.

"You know, you should sell your bars to the bakeries in town," I tell Francine on Friday afternoon, trying to figure out which bar is the biggest. We've just finished our last official rehearsal day at Auburn. Renee had to go to a doctor's appointment, so her mom picked her up as soon as we were done singing, and Eric's family was going to pick out a tree (lucky), so he had already left, too. Matthew and I were in the lobby with Francine, figuring we'd earned a treat after so much singing.

Matthew, Eric, Renee, and I will meet again over the weekend to finalize our audition, but we've practiced as much as we can. Which is to say that we've sung together as a group a lot, but we don't really have much of a plan. I'm trying to focus on the sweet chocolatey goodness and not on the fact that . . . we probably won't get the spotlight.

"Oh, you're sweet, honey," Francine says, patting my cheek gently with her palm. Her skin is silky smooth and it makes me think of how I can't wait to see my grandmother.

"Charlie, they have something similar at the Daily Grind," Matthew says.

"Matthew Yee," Francine says. Her back straightens, which brings her up a few inches. "Are you suggesting that those bars are comparable to the ones I make for you upstairs in my own kitchen?"

"No, ma'am," Matthew says quickly. "I didn't . . . I mean, I wasn't trying to . . ."

It's pretty hilarious to watch the usually very poised Matthew flail.

I catch the twinkle in Francine's eye just before she begins to speak.

"Well," she says, the gruffness in her tone belying those twinkling eyes. "Maybe you should bring Charlie there to test them out. I know she'll tell me the truth."

Oh my goodness. Is Francine trying to . . . ? No. Maybe. Gulp.

"Oh, you don't need to take me there, Matthew," I say quickly. "I'm sure Francine's are better."

But Matthew raises his eyebrows. "Well, I think you should keep an open mind. Maybe the Daily Grind can hold their own."

"It's worth investigating." Francine begins to walk away. "I'll expect a full report on Monday. You're going to come back and tell me how the audition went anyway, right?"

"Right," I echo, barely thinking of the audition now. I can't meet Matthew's gaze. Did he know . . . was he going along with . . .

Matthew pushes a hand through his straight dark hair. "Well, I was just going to walk home. But want to stop by the Daily Grind with me on the way?" While Matthew's eyes are laughing, there's also something serious in there. Like he's almost . . . nervous?

"You don't have to," I stumble.

"But I want to."

Oh. "Okay." I whisper. "Can I meet you outside?"

I dial Renee as I scurry away.

"What did I forget?" she asks, without greeting me.

"Um." I can't breathe. Maybe Matthew feels he has to bring me to the Daily Grind because Francine basically forced his hand.

"Charlie?"

That's the thing about talking on the phone. You actually need to talk. I really should have just texted her. Except, my fingers feel very shaky. "Um . . ." I start again. "Matthew invited me to go to the Daily Grind with him. But it's kind of because . . ." And then I blurt out the whole story, whispering just in case Matthew finishes saying good-bye to his grandparents before I've gotten through it.

Renee laughs. "Well, definitely tell me how it goes. Listen, I'm at the doctor. Can we talk later?"

"No, I need . . ." I'm panicking. Full-on panicking. What does this mean? Do I want to do this? Does this mean something? Is it a *date*?

"You'll be fine. I have to go." I hear Renee's mom in the background, telling Renee to shut off the phone or she'll shut it off for her, which is the only reason I don't call back. That and the fact that Matthew is making his way through the front doors.

"Ready?" he asks, wrapping his scarf around his neck.

"Yup!" I lie, and we're off.

By the time we're seated at the Daily Grind, I can barely feel my cheeks, they're so cold. My eyes feel like they froze while we walked, though I'm not sure if eyeballs can technically freeze. Either way, my hands are warming against the mug of hot chocolate I have in front of me, and I'm trying to defrost my face with the steam.

Ironically, today of all days, the Daily Grind was out of the chocolate brownie bars. I thought maybe Matthew would see that as a reason for us to ditch the plan, but it didn't seem to have an impact on him at all. Instead, he ordered two chocolate chip cookies for us to share, and I got us two mugs of hot cocoa with whipped cream.

"I'm so glad you ordered hot chocolate," Matthew says. His glasses are completely fogged up, so I can't imagine he can see me at all. It must be annoying to wear glasses, though on him, they look really cute.

"I was worried you'd laugh at me, but I don't like coffee." I wrinkle my nose, and he laughs.

"I don't like coffee either," he says, and my whole body lightens. "Sometimes if I'm feeling really tired, I order a mocha, but then I have to add a ton of sugar and extra milk and it still makes me hyper and tastes bitter."

He's back to talking a mile a minute, and I love this new nervous Matthew. It almost makes him feel more real. Not that he didn't seem real before. He's definitely real. But this way he feels more approachable.

More like me.

"Do you come to this place often?" I ask, and I have to

swallow a giggle because it sounds like a line from a movie: *Come here often?* with an eyebrow waggle.

Apparently, swallowing giggles makes me cough a lot. Which shakes the table. And the hot chocolate. Luckily, Matthew grabs both mugs while I hack to the side.

"Don't worry, I'm not sick," I gasp, and that makes me laugh even more because of course he knows I'm not sick. We've spent every day together.

I'm not mature enough for a coffee date, apparently. Not that this is definitely a date. I mean, it's really just an opportunity to warm up on a cold day. Or . . .

"Are you okay?" Matthew's leaning over the table, still holding the mugs, but it means his face is even closer to mine than before. Especially when I lift my head.

Our faces are really, really close together.

"I'm fine," I squeak. I try to take a deep breath to calm myself, but it's hard to breathe like that with Matthew so close. Why is he so close? Is he going to kiss me? No. That's totally not possible. I mean, I don't even know if he likes me. Or if I like him.

Actually, that's not true. I may not know if he likes me, but I know I like him. Which is so scary to admit that any ground I've gained in breathing is lost again.

"Do you want some water?" he asks, and I nod.

I like Matthew Yee.

I like Matthew Yee.

Each time I say it in my head, I know it's more true, and I feel more panicked.

This is nothing like having a crush on Eric. Eric is cute and sweet and a good friend, but this . . . feels different. It feels scarier. Having a crush on Eric felt like I needed to convince him that he liked me. This is different.

So different.

Thank goodness the counter is busy. It's taking time for Matthew to get the barista's attention to ask for water, and that gives me a chance to grab my phone and text Renee.

Me: OMG. Help!

It feels like it takes forever before I see that she's texting back.

Renee: Why help?

Me: I think—I glance over to the counter; Matthew is still waiting—I like him.

I debate whether to press SEND but he's getting closer and closer to the front of the line and I need to know what Renee thinks. So I shut my eyes and press SEND.

Holding my breath, I open my eyes to check my phone. I can see that she's typing her response, but Matthew is also walking toward me with a cup of water.

Come on, come on, I beg Renee silently. It's like she starts and stops typing, and I can't imagine what she's going to tell me. She couldn't be telling me to leave, right? Or maybe she's warning me that she knows what he's doing. That this is a practical joke, and she wants me to know there are cameras hidden to see if I fall for the trick, the trick that Matthew Yee might like me back. I can't breathe. I can't—

The text comes through. One word.

Renee: Duh.

"Here's your water," Matthew says. "Sorry about the wait, but they're really busy up there."

I drop my phone into my bag and try to appear relaxed.

What did she mean by *duh*? Like everyone knows I like him? Or maybe it was some weird autocorrect for something else. Like *don't*.

Just then, my phone pings again. I ignore it because what if it's Renee and she says something really embarrassing like *JUST KISS HIM* and Matthew sees it when I pick it up?

Or what if it says, *He's out of your league*?

My phone pings *again*, and apparently I'm smiling like a crazy person ignoring her phone because Matthew is giving me one of those *If I could, I'd back away slowly* looks. When it pings for the third time, I finally grab it.

It's my mom. She'll be here in ten minutes.

Ten minutes. I've wasted most of this coffee date worrying. Not-date. Coffee—hot chocolate—thing.

But I have ten minutes. I send Mom back a thumbs-up, and slide my phone into my bag, jiggling it around so that it's on the bottom, so any pinging won't be a distraction.

"Sorry," I tell Matthew. "My mom is picking me up in ten minutes."

Is it my imagination or does he look a little disappointed? "No prob."

All around us, there's chattering and the clinking of spoons against coffee cups. I blow softly on the hot chocolate and then dip in a spoon, lifting the whipped cream to my mouth in a big bite. Mmm.

Matthew is taking a sip of his hot cocoa, too, and when he puts his mug down, he has some whipped cream on his upper lip.

I try not to laugh. "Um . . ." I motion to his lip.

"What?" He frowns, looking confused.

You're adorable, I want to say, but don't. Instead, feeling brave, I lean forward and quickly swipe the whipped cream off with my thumb. My face is burning, and I could swear Matthew is blushing, too.

"Thanks," he says with a laugh, but I can tell he's a little embarrassed.

I stir my cocoa and try to think of something—anything—to say. Or, rather, anything reasonable.

"Francine is a riot," I blurt out.

Matthew smiles. "She's something. Did I tell you that my grandma says that she's trying to get the building to allow pets for therapeutic reasons?"

Francine with all her schemes. "But isn't she allergic to dogs and cats?"

She'd told me that during her mammoth debrief on everything there was to know about her life, earlier in our visits.

She'd told me matter-of-factly that when she was growing up, she'd always wanted a cat, but there was barely enough food on the table for her family, and her mother had scoffed at the idea of another mouth to feed. And how disappointed she was as an adult when she found out that even with enough food to feed her family, she was too allergic to fluffy animals to have one of her own.

"She wants to get a parrot on the basis that it would talk with her and she wouldn't feel so lonely," Matthew explains.

There's something hilarious about the idea of tiny Francine with a parrot on her shoulder, walking down the corridors of the senior home. How Mr. Carlson will shake his head, sigh that *it's just not right*. How after she walks by, a swing in her step, he'll secretly smile.

"It's going to be weird not going there to rehearse." Even I can hear the hitch in my voice, and I lower my head so Matthew won't be able to tell that my eyes are filling with tears.

How can I give up seeing Francine and Mr. and Mrs. Yee? Matthew's grandparents are always so kind, always dressed up so nicely, offering us tea and cookies. I'm going to miss the way they stare at Matthew when they think he's not watching, beaming.

"I think they'd be sad if we didn't come back. In fact, they have a little bet going."

There's a lightness in Matthew's voice that helps me push back the tears, blink them away. "What kind of bet? Like about the show?"

"No," he laughs, and I can't help it, I meet his eyes. "They think there's a secret romance going on in our little group."

The warmth that's filling me has nothing to do with the hot chocolate and the cozy café and everything to do with Matthew's words and the way he's staring at me.

"Um, what do you mean?"

My heart is pounding in my ears, and I'm suddenly afraid of what he'll say. What if—

"They think that Eric is secretly in love with Renee. The bet is whether or not he'll tell her by the night of the performance."

His voice has now gone serious, and his eyes have questions in them. But it's hard to think because I'm reeling from what he just said, the distance between that and what I wished he'd said. Or maybe I don't care. Maybe this is all in my head.

"I told them that I thought maybe he was interested in you."

I sputter and shake my head, and I don't even know how to feel, what to think. I don't know what Matthew is trying to say.

"Eric isn't interested in me," I whisper, finally admitting it to myself. And I realize I'm okay with it. "We're friends. That's the only way he's ever thought of me. And I'm quite sure that's how Renee thinks of him as well."

I'd be okay if Renee liked Eric, I realize, and not just because I know she's not interested in him like that. If that ever changes, I'll make sure to tell her that whatever I felt for Eric is long gone.

"I think . . ." Matthew pauses and fills his lungs with air. And just then my phone pings. Even though it's in the dark recesses of my bag where I can't even find it, I can hear it ping. And then I hear the honk from outside, and spot my mom's car.

I want to ask Matthew what he thinks. I want to know whether it's something about me and Eric, or me and him. Or maybe Eric and Renee. I want to know and yet it's so much safer not knowing. Because once you know, you can't un-know it. And then you have to deal with the consequences.

Ignoring Matthew, I rise out of my seat and wave at my mom across the street. I drink down the last of my hot chocolate, and then tip it back to get a little bit more. God, that chocolate was amazing.

"Do you want me to ask if she can drive you home also?" I ask, pretending that there isn't this huge thing floating between us. All these questions and an interrupted *I think*.

"I'm good," he says. "My mom will be here soon."

I flip on my coat, trying desperately not to smack anyone with my scarf and all my layers. It's snowing again, and the windows are slightly steamed, and I can't believe that Matthew Yee and I went out for hot chocolate in this cute little café as it snowed outside. It's probably the most romantic thing that's ever happened to me and I spent the whole time worrying.

Typical.

"Thank you," I whisper because once again I'm an emotional mess. "This was really fun."

Matthew grins. "Next time you'll have to get that chocolate brownie bar. It's really *so* good!"

I nod and wonder about his words as I maneuver through the crowded café. Did he mean next time we come here together, or next time I come here by myself?

Boys are just too complicated.

Chapter Fifteen

It's the day of the big audition, and the hallway is filled with carolers. Technically, there are only sixteen of us, but for some reason, it feels like many more right now.

Maybe it's because I'm finding it hard to breathe.

Renee's fingers are clasped in mine, and based on the way she's wincing every so often, I think I might be holding on too tight. But when I ask her if I'm crushing her hand, she shakes her head.

We aren't ready.

I know anything can happen, and I know we've practiced as much as we can, but I also know that we've been distracted.

I've been distracted.

I glance over to Matthew, who is in the middle of an animated conversation with Eric, and I can't believe that three weeks ago, the thought of having to sing with him made me annoyed. Three weeks ago, I could barely talk to Eric without stuttering, and I thought the only thing that was important was winning the solo.

I let go of Renee and wipe my palms on my skirt, try to calm my breathing. Did what I want change or did I let myself get distracted? Am I going to miss my chance to finally sing onstage, all eyes on me, just because a cute boy with floppy hair paid attention to me?

Or did I decide getting the solo didn't matter as much as I thought it did?

We're the last to be called. When Mrs. Hamilton finally asks us into the room, it doesn't feel like I'm walking into the audition of my life. It feels like Renee is dragging me inside.

We don't have this.

"Hey, Charlie, Renee, Eric, and Matthew!" Mrs. Hamilton gives each of us a high five, her special thing, and then nods down at the car seat in front of her. "I'm sorry that Ethan's appearance threw a wrench into all our plans."

The baby bundled up in the carrier doesn't look like the type to cause major problems. All I can see is his little face, his pink lips pursed together.

"He's beautiful," I say, and as he starts shifting, Mrs. Hamilton rocks the seat lightly until he settles back.

"Thank you. And thank you for finding a solution to the rehearsing issue."

"Which rehearsing solution?" Eric chimes in. "We've had a few now."

Mrs. Hamilton marvels as we explain the places we've had to rehearse, our different audiences.

"Well," she finally says when we're through. "Let's hear what you've got!"

We got inspired by singing at Auburn, so we changed up our song list a little. It's mostly the same as what we'd begun by singing on the street corners, but with the tempo we developed during our afternoons at Auburn. More old-fashioned than pop. We sound good but we make some mistakes, and I can read our every misstep on Mrs. Hamilton's face.

But still we sing our hearts out. We perform "The Little Drummer Boy" slowly, the way Francine's mom used to like it, and then we sing "Silent Night" the way the folks at Auburn requested it. And when it comes to "Let It Go," Renee and Eric sing it the way they'd done it that first day on the street, though with a little less shivering from all of us. And "Hanukkah, O Hanukkah" sounds just like it did when we sang it at Renee's Hanukkah party: playful and fun, and a perfect segue into our final song: my duet with Eric of "Blue Christmas." My eyes fill with tears and my voice grows thick, but I can't help it. What if this is the last time we're singing together?

What if things go back to the way they used to be when this is all over?

"Thank you so much," Mrs. Hamilton says as the last notes dissolve. The four of us join hands and take a little bow, and I don't think I'm imagining that Matthew's grip on my hand is as tight as mine is on Renee's.

"Do you have a minute?" Matthew asks Mrs. Hamilton. "I had a question."

It's over. It's over.

"I have to go," I whisper to nobody in particular as Matthew starts talking to Mrs. Hamilton, as Eric and Renee confer in the corner. I use the lack of attention to race out of the room before the tears can make their way down my cheeks.

Renee: Where are you?

Renee: Where are you?

Renee: If you don't text me back, I'm calling the police. Or your mom.

Renee's texts are coming fast and furious.

I stare at my phone. I can't figure out which is more likely: that Renee would call the police or my mom. Either way, I know I'm being ridiculous. Especially since I'm sitting in a bathroom stall, which is all kinds of ick. Zombie apocalypse? I might be patient zero.

Me: I'm fine

Renee: Where are you? I'm searching this dumb school on crutches and my leg hurts.

I snort a laugh. Renee has become so strong on her crutches, my guess is that if she's with Eric and Matthew, she's leaving them in the dust.

Matthew. And Eric. I didn't say good-bye to them. I just ran.

Me: I need a little time on my own.

Renee: That's nice, dear, but it's not happening. Eric's dad just took the boys to Auburn and my mom is waiting for us outside. I'll sit in the front and you can mope in the back, but you're coming.

Shoot. I don't want to go. I don't want to face anyone. I failed.

Another text comes in.

Renee: Now.

I move.

Renee is true to her word, and she doesn't try to engage me in conversation during the short drive to Auburn. I'm not sure what she's told her mom, but even Mrs. Levine doesn't ask questions. The silence lasts until we're inside the building, moving toward the atrium. Except, instead of just our regular crowd, there's a larger than usual number of people congregated near our makeshift stage. Eric's parents are there, as well as Matthew's and Matthew's grandparents, and Francine and Hank. And even my parents and Sadie.

And Mrs. Hamilton.

What's Mrs. Hamilton doing here?

"Hey!" Matthew smiles when he sees us approaching. He nods at his grandfather and then in two long strides he's in front of us.

"Hey," I mumble, my hair falling forward to cover my face. I can't believe I ran like that. Matthew must think—

"I hope you aren't mad at me," Matthew says, and he glances over at Renee, who gives him a nod. He's talking quickly, so I know he's nervous. "I've been talking with the other groups over the past few days, and everyone really loved singing in their quartets. Anna's group did a whole medley just of Hanukkah songs, and Evan's group did Christmas carols in different languages. And Phoebe's group found some really interesting old carols that I'd never even heard of."

His voice conveys how impressed he was, and it makes me feel even worse. We weren't as creative as those other groups. Even if I'd known deep down that we didn't have a shot, any tiny thread of hope just dissolved. I wrap my arms around my middle.

"I was talking with Mrs. Hamilton after our audition, and I suggested a new plan. The truth is that, apart from a couple of songs that we all know really well, we haven't practiced as a chorus since before Thanksgiving. Which means we probably won't sound all that good unless someone is willing to work with us every day after school until the concert. And there's nobody who can do that."

He takes a deep breath, and I realize it's the first time I've heard the intake of air since he started talking. He really cares about this. It's so clear now.

"So I recommended to Mrs. Hamilton that we change the holiday concert. All four quartets would be able to perform, because she thought that we were all equally strong. Or maybe strong in different ways." His voice deepens on those last words, and I gulp. We were strong? He nods, as though he could hear my thoughts. "Instead of doing the usual concert at school, I proposed we do a caroling event here, at Auburn, as a way of thanking them for hosting us and as a way of bringing the holiday music out where people need it. The chorus would start off with one carol and then each group will perform on their own, and then the chorus will finish all together."

This wasn't making any sense. The holiday concert wouldn't be a real chorus concert with soloists or a concert with a special performance. It would be a series of performances, and it would be here?

"But there's no stage?" I can hear the ridiculousness in the question as soon as it leaves my lips.

"Nope," Matthew says with a grin. "There isn't. But the chorus has sixteen fantastic singers and we can use this makeshift stage. And there's plenty of room for an audience and all our families."

At that, I turn to my parents, who are chatting with Francine.

I try not to let the hurt zing through me. "That's not going to be a big deal for me because my parents are going away."

"Yup," says Matthew with a grin, and I'm starting to get freaked out by this happy, grinning Matthew. Who is he? "They're going away on Friday morning. But, luckily, Auburn wants us to perform here on Thursday night. So not only will your parents be in the audience, but so will your grandparents, since their train will be here by showtime."

This time his grin is infectious and I can't help but get caught up in it. Wait, how does he know all this stuff? And why?

"Why did you do all this?" I blurt. "Chorus isn't even really your thing. Neither is Christmas, I guess?"

"True, I don't love Christmas as much as you do," he says, and the laughing is gone from his voice. "Or chorus for that matter. But these past weeks of rehearsing together have really shown me the difference holiday songs make in people's lives. How it reminds them of where they come from. How it brings people happiness. How it brings people together."

He takes a small step forward and my heart rate accelerates so fast I'm worried that everyone can hear it. But when he looks at me that way, I don't notice anything but him and his warm dark eyes. There's noise all around us but it's just noise.

"Thank you," I whisper.

"It's going to be fun," he chuckles. "I've learned that we have fun wherever we go, Charlie Dickens."

And I realize then that he was never making fun of me when he said my whole name. He just likes my name.

And maybe . . . just maybe . . . me?

Chapter Sixteen

"How many people are out there?" I whisper to Renee. I've been hiding in one of the back corridors, checking singers in on my spreadsheet, mostly because I'm worried that we won't have an audience. Which is fine, I keep reminding myself. Even if there are only ten of our regulars, and double that in performers, it's totally fine.

The past four days have been madness. All the quartets were on board for the Auburn performance, and Mrs. Hamilton even came in yesterday after school so we could rehearse as a chorus. It wasn't our best rehearsal, but the good news is that we can only get better.

"I think we're going to need to start early," Renee whispers back.

"Do people look bored?" I cringe.

"No. But I don't think there's much more room to be had."

"But that's not possible," I say, slipping past her. "The atrium is huge and . . . oh my god."

Renee is right. The atrium is full. There must be hundreds of people here. From my vantage point behind the makeshift stage, I can see the chairs that we reserved for the buildings' residents are full, as are the rows behind them for the singers' families. And beyond that . . . there are so many people. People from town, kids from the elementary and high school, everyone.

"Wow," I whisper.

"Look, your mom and dad are waving!" Renee calls.

Well, Mom is waving. Dad has a tripod set up with the video camera trained on the exact spot where I'll be. He asked me a few times, and then asked again just to confirm. Sadie and Jed are out there, too, as are my grandparents. My heart fills with a warm glow at the sight of them.

"I think it's time to start." While it doesn't surprise me that I can recognize Matthew's voice even from behind me, what does surprise me is how familiar it is, how familiar he has become. We've been working nonstop on the concert, spending hours and hours every night arranging details. And while there's been a closeness . . . we haven't talked about it. Because even if it's just as friends, that's okay, too. Turns out popular star athletes can be really awesome friends. If they aren't interested in being more.

"Let's do it," I whisper.

Mrs. Hamilton takes the stage and welcomes everyone, explaining the genesis of the concert. When she mentions our quartet in particular and how much we'd done to save the concert, the applause is almost deafening. I beam and squeeze Renee's hand. Matthew is on the other side of the stage, going over the final lighting instructions, so I can't take his hand, too. Though he looks up when he hears our names and his wink makes my heart soar.

The concert goes as Matthew had laid it out on Monday. Each group gets four songs, and the chorus opens and closes the show, plus one song in the middle. I'd debated whether I wanted us to go first or be stuck in the middle or go last, but I finally put it in Renee and Eric's hands since they were coordinating the various groups. At first I asked them not to tell me, but then this morning I caved.

"Last," Renee said with a twinkle in her eye.

"Ugh," I groaned. "That's a lot of pressure."

"Remember, there's still the finale," she laughs.

The finale. That was the biggest surprise. Instead of closing with a classic song, or even a new popular one, Mrs. Hamilton gave us a new song to learn. At yesterday's rehearsal, it was the one we practiced over and over until it was so ingrained in our brains that I could hear bits of the melody wherever I went.

Mrs. Hamilton had told us it was written by a friend of hers, that this would be its world premiere. At first I was hesitant about it: Why couldn't we do a song we already knew?

But once we sang it the first time, I could see why Mrs. Hamilton chose it. It had the same multicultural feeling as the songs that made up the concert now, but also felt classic, like the elderly people at Auburn would appreciate it. And . . . I couldn't place it. But it felt familiar.

"Is it from a movie?" I asked Mrs. Hamilton. She shook her head.

"Don't worry about where the song came from. I think it's a perfect way to end the concert."

And there was nobody who disagreed. Especially since it had a great beat to it.

We begin as a chorus with "It's the Most Wonderful Time of the Year," and it's the perfect beginning since we're feeling it. All of us. We may not be Pentatonix, but there's something about the way we all worked so hard on making this happen that our bodies are loose and our voices . . . sound good.

Really, really good.

Anna's group and Phoebe's follow, and I have to admit that Matthew wasn't kidding when he said they'd done some incredible work. I even have tears in my eyes as I glance out into the audience and see Renee's grandfather singing along to a Hanukkah song in Ladino. I nudge Renee only to find that she has tears in her eyes, too.

We regroup as a chorus for "Walking in a Winter Wonderland," and the song reminds me of skating around the rink (*before* the accident), of sledding with Matthew, of our hot chocolate date. I see Dad filming and I'm going to be too embarrassed ever to watch this video, because I'm sure I'm grinning like a fool.

Then it's Evan's group, and they use little flags as props for each song, and they have the audience eating out of their hands.

"Ready?" Renee asks as they take their bows.

"It's now or never," I whisper, and the two of us walk out onstage to meet Matthew and Eric.

While our scarves aren't homemade, I'm sure we make cute carolers in our coats with matching hats. We even stand as I'd asked them to, hands clasped in front. There's a brief second before we start, and I glance over at Matthew. "Thank you," I whisper, and then we're off.

If we'd made any mistakes during our audition with Mrs. Hamilton, they were our last ones. Because our performance is flawless. And when it comes to "The Little Drummer Boy," it's exactly as it was my dream. Even if it isn't onstage at the school.

And it isn't Eric who holds my hand unexpectedly. It's Matthew. I wasn't prepared for the zing when he takes my hand, and it almost breaks my concentration. Then, if anything, it only strengthens it.

When the applause rains down, I don't think I'm fooling myself that we receive the most of any group. But truthfully,

I don't really care. My parents are beaming from the front row, and I've just sung my heart out.

It's an amazing night. And it ends perfectly with Mrs. Hamilton's special song. Even though it's new and unfamiliar to everyone in the audience, they are completely into it, clapping and snapping along. And for some reason, whether it's the tune or rhythm or lyrics or something else, there's a difference in us when we sing it. We're still not anything like PTX, but . . . we're getting closer.

And when it's over, I want to cry. But not from sadness. Not at all.

We did it.

Chapter Seventeen

When the knock comes on Friday afternoon, I'm finishing up my hot chocolate display. I had to wait until Mom and Dad left so that I could commandeer the counter space. Technically, I probably should have asked, but it was just piles of old mail, bowls that didn't fit anywhere else, and Dad's virtually unused Mixmaster. Not that I had anywhere to put all that stuff. But that was a problem for later.

Grandma and I had carefully cleaned all the giant jars we'd bought, and I set up the mini signs describing all the hot chocolate fixings: marshmallows, candy canes, caramel sauce, sprinkles, whipped cream, sea salt, coffee, and more.

I might have gone a little overboard. But the fake chalkboard was so pretty and the whole thing looked . . . kind of fabulous.

Which is why I was smiling when I opened the door.

Not because I knew it was Matthew.

"Hey." His smile is more tentative, and I can't believe I ever thought he was full of himself. The truth is, he has a lot of friends because he's a good guy. And he works hard on the basketball court and in school, which is why he's the captain and gets good grades.

I'd been silly, thinking that just because he was popular, he must be shallow.

"Can I come in?" he asks, and I choke out a laugh.

"Sorry! Of course." He slips off his shoes at the door, revealing multicolored socks with reindeer on them. I might be in love. They're so adorable. He's so adorable. "Nice socks," I eke out.

He chuckles as he hangs his dark blue peacoat on the hook and follows me into the kitchen.

In an ironic turn of fate, school was canceled today. Early this morning, a pipe burst from the cold, flooding the auditorium and some of the classrooms in the science wing. If it had been earlier in the semester, they probably would have found some solution for us to be able to attend school. But since it was the last day before break, they just gave the entire middle school an extra day of winter vacation. I'm sure the Space Station could hear our cheers, particularly given how late we all got home from the concert last night.

But the part that I couldn't stop thinking about was how, if we hadn't changed the concert date and location, there wouldn't have been a concert. The flooded auditorium would have ruined everything.

All that hard work would have gone for nothing.

So Auburn ended up being our little miracle.

"You must be Matthew," my grandmother says from the kitchen table. As I'd been finishing the hot chocolate display, she'd been creating shopping lists based on our extensive pile of cookie recipes. "You did a beautiful job at the holiday concert yesterday."

Matthew blushes and stutters out a thank you. "I'm sorry I didn't get to meet you last night," he says. "Charlie talks about you a lot."

"You are so sweet," Grandma says, and sends me a wink.

Now it's my turn to blush, hoping against hope that Matthew didn't see that little sign.

"Charlie, why don't you offer Matthew some hot chocolate?" Grandma says, standing up. "I'm going to go check on the yarn I brought for your knitting project and see how your grandfather is doing reading with Sadie."

Ever since the conversation with Matthew that night when he stayed for dinner, Sadie has been a little calmer about the work she's doing with the reading specialist. While she used to frown on anything involving books, thanks to Matthew's suggestion, she's now agreed to give audiobooks a chance. Which is awesome. The fact that

232

she's getting interested in stories has been motivating her to do whatever it takes to learn to read. Even if that means testing and working with a tutor. For Christmas, my grandparents ordered her a whole load of audiobooks, but since they haven't come in the mail yet, my grandfather has spent the morning reading out loud to her, which she's loved.

And which has given me uninterrupted time with Grandma.

"Love you," I whisper to my grandmother as she gives me a hug.

"He seems like a nice boy," she whispers back, and then she quickly leaves the kitchen.

Please let Matthew not have heard any of that! "Oh, wow," Matthew says when he sees my little display. Or maybe it's because it looks like Pinterest just exploded all over my kitchen.

I may have gone a little overboard.

"Hot chocolate?" I offer, and he nods in rapt attention.

"Wow," he says again when I hand him the sugary confection. "This is delicious. Between you and Francine, you could open a café."

"You don't think the hot chocolate at the Daily Grind is better?" I tease, and he flushes.

"Definitely not." We sit in silence in the kitchen, enjoying our drinks (third hot chocolate of the day for me—this time with the caramel and sea salt. YUM!).

"So I brought you a Christmas present," Matthew says, his words spoken practically directly into his hot chocolate.

I squeal before I can stop myself. "You didn't need to." I glance around him and it must be small, because otherwise I can't see it.

"I wanted to." He shrugs.

"Okay, then let me get yours." I dash upstairs before he has a chance to say anything and race into my room.

This morning, in addition to decorating with my grandmother and making the hot chocolate bar, I made presents for Eric, Renee, and Matthew. I still have to work on my family ones, but I have until Christmas for those.

I grab Matthew's gift, a little nervous about how he'll take it.

When I'd initially had the idea for the hot chocolate bar, I'd gone out to find some plain white mugs from the dollar store. I figured I'd put little chalkboard labels on them and use them for our special Christmas mugs. But this morning, I realized that we didn't need special mugs for our hot chocolate bar. Instead, I wanted to bring the hot chocolate bar to others.

And so in each mug, I put a couple of servings of hot cocoa, a few marshmallows, some crushed-up candy canes for mint, and a little packet of caramel and sea salt. The whipped cream they'd have to take care of themselves.

The only one I'd been unsure of was Matthew's mug. Because while I could say that his gift was like everyone else's, there was something special about giving him hot chocolate, because it reminded me of our date/not-date at the Daily Grind. And because this morning I'd been feeling brave, I'd taken out my special markers and carefully drew THE DAILY GRIND logo on it, decorating it to look as authentic as possible.

And then at the last minute, I made one for myself also. I told myself it was so I could give the better version to Matthew, but it was really because I wanted my own. He'd never know it, but I wanted a matching one.

But now I feel like maybe the whole thing is too much. Like maybe it will embarrass him and then he'll feel awkward around me and . . .

Standing outside the kitchen, I debate going back and grabbing one of the plain ones, when I glance inside and see Matthew pacing back and forth.

And suddenly it feels okay to be nervous, because this boy just came to my house to deliver a Christmas present and he was most definitely nervous as well.

I place the wrapped mug on the kitchen island and the sound stops his pacing. His eyes are sheepish, and I try to tell him with mine that I'm also nervous. And also scared. And also . . .

"Can I go first?" I ask, and he nods.

I slide the mug over to him, and my heart warms as he picks it up, cradling it in his hand. "You need to make sure not to put it in the dishwasher," I say, "because the marker might start to fade. And if you don't like it, I have a plain mug. Or—"

I'm babbling. Full-on babbling.

"It's awesome." His grin is wide, and I wonder how anyone can stand near him and not smile. "Thank you."

"You're welcome."

There's a long pause, and I swallow. Maybe my gift is too much and now he feels bad or maybe it's not enough, like he bought me something and is now rethinking it or—

"So, um . . ." He turns toward the window, and my gaze follows his to the snow falling outside. "For the past few weeks, you've said a bunch of times that you didn't know why I was doing all this chorus stuff, because I'm not a singer."

"No, that's—" I begin, but he shakes his head. I want to hide my face, I'm so embarrassed. I want to tell him that I didn't know then. That I don't think that anymore. That it's not a contest of who likes it best.

"And I think that's my fault. Because I didn't tell you. I know that I'm not the most talented singer, but singing is important to me. Or, rather—"

"You don't have to—" I begin again, but he frowns.

"Do you want your present?" he asks, and I'm relieved to hear the slight teasing back in his voice.

"Sorry," I murmur.

"I joined chorus not because of the singing, but because I love songs. I love listening to music and hearing how voices come together. And more than that, I love writing songs."

He stops there and those last four words hang in the air between us.

"The song we sang last night? The finale? That was my song." He gulps and I want to say something, but all my words are lost. "I asked Mrs. Hamilton not to tell anyone because I was too embarrassed and too nervous that people would hate it. And then when everyone loved it, I . . . I wanted it to be my secret. I liked it that way."

He takes a deep breath, and then meets my eyes. "Except, I did want you to know. Because I thought of you a lot when I was writing it. And there was one verse that I didn't want us to sing last night because it was too personal. And because you'd know it was me who'd written it as soon as you heard it."

Oh. Oh. Oh. I can't breathe. I can't—

"Can I sing it to you?"

My head bobs, a much smaller movement than I really want to make. I want to jump up and down screaming but my limbs don't really work right now.

Matthew Yee wrote last night's song. And he thought of me. And . . .

He coughs once and takes a deep breath and exhales. He turns back to the window, and it's perfect because now I see us reflected in the windowpanes against the snow falling in the dark backyard, the twinkling of Christmas lights behind us.

In every tale of winter cheer,

There's holiday joy, and friends so near.

There's snow-covered hills, sleds flying fast,

Skating hand in hand on days that last.

But every so often, over hot chocolate and a glance,

Something changes and there's a chance

Of a very special Christmas.

I want to say something.

I want to breathe or smile or shout or cry or . . .

Matthew wrote that song. Matthew wrote that song, and he said he'd been thinking of me and there's a verse that . . .

"The song is so beautiful." Even to my own ears, I can hear the astonishment in my voice, the pride. "You wrote that?"

Matthew's chin dips a little, and I can't help it. I should just stay still, but I can't. My hand finds itself on his arm and I don't know how it got there, but there was no place else it could go.

"I've been writing songs for a while," he admits.

"You're really talented."

Slowly, I feel the world come back around us. The snow falling. The twinkling lights. The smell of the hot chocolate.

"Was that song my gift?" At first I'm worried that it sounds like I don't think it's enough, but the way his lips curl up, I know he hears the awe in my question.

"It's the best gift I could imagine," I say. I think about gifts that fit under the tree, and what my parents mean when they talk about experience gifts. They're right. The things I remember aren't the things in boxes that came from others, but things like this.

Something that is given from the heart.

"I'm a little embarrassed by my gift," I mutter. "It's not as special as—"

"I love it," he says quickly. "You know how I feel about hot chocolate. And I'll always remember that day at the Daily Grind."

"Me too."

There's so much filling the room right now. So much emotion, so much happiness spilling out of me. I'm overheating, but it feels okay this time. It feels nice. And I don't want it to stop.

"Remember how you said that I should try the chocolate brownies at the Daily Grind?" I don't pause long enough for him to answer. "Well, I was wondering if maybe you wanted to go back to the Daily Grind with me one day again."

The realization of what I've just said hits me with full force and I'm about to turn four shades of bright red.

"I would like that," he whispers.

"Me too," I agree. "I think I'd like that a lot."

There's a long pause and we're inching closer and closer, and his eyes are on mine. "I'd really like to kiss you right now." His words are so quiet, I almost think they're just my thoughts, but then he adds: "If it would be okay with you?"

I nod, very emphatically. And then he leans forward and there's a faint brush of his lips against mine. And I think this is something I'm going to want to do again.

CREATE YOUR OWN HOT CHOCOLATE BAR

Hot chocolate bars really should be a year-round project, because there's never a bad time for a nice cup of hot cocoa. There are many ways to create your own, but here's Charlie's technique.

Equipment:

- Hot chocolate powder. You can use a store bought variety or mix your own. There are many great recipes online.
- Hot chocolate extras: Mini marshmallows, candy canes (mini or big), sea salt, Mexican spice mix, cinnamon, instant coffee, pretzels, maraschino cherries, coconut flakes, etc.
- Squeeze bottles/canisters of whipped cream, caramel sauce, butterscotch sauce, chocolate sauce (there's never too much chocolate)
- Jars with lids—as many as you have toppings (mason/canning jars are a great inexpensive option)
- Spoons and scoops

- Labels (chalkboard stickers are great, but regular labels are also good in a pinch)
- Paper for decorating squeeze bottles and canisters

Directions:

1. Once you have all your equipment, it's just a matter of finding a nice spot and creating your labels. You can put down pretty cloth napkins to really frame your spot, or a nice tray. Get creative and lay down a few springs of holly or a small vase of flowers.

2. For the labels: If you are already using chalkboard labels, then just practice your best handwriting to create signs for what's in each jar. If you are using regular labels or taping paper, you can turn to one of the many free online picture-creating tools and create "fake" chalkboard labels. With this option, you can use pretty handwriting fonts so you don't need to worry about smudges or mistakes.

Enjoy! Don't forget to refrigerate your perishable supplies (like the whipped cream!) and ask for help making the hot chocolate on the stove.

HOT CHOCOLATE BAR TO GO!

While the display is pretty, this can also become a cute gift for Christmas or any time.

1. Pick up some plain mugs at the dollar store, and add a chalkboard label. For these gifts, having real chalkboard labels is important so that the label will stick on the mug even after it's been washed.

2. Fill a little bag with cocoa mix (the amount needed for one serving), and add in a few extras (like a candy cane and a piece of caramel), and then a cute list of doctored-up hot chocolate recipes (peppermint mocha is always a good one!).

3. Write your friend's name or a cute quote on the label, and add a small piece of chalk so they can also create their own messages.

Acknowledgments

There are so many people who deserve the kudos for making this book possible. First and foremost to Aimee Friedman, editor extraordinaire and secret twin. I never would have imagined that this would have been our first book together. I'm looking forward to many, many more.

And to Rena Bunder Rossner, who always has my back and makes things happen in the most fabulous ways.

The team at Scholastic has been a dream to work with. Thank you to Jennifer Rinaldi, Jael Fogle, Ann Marie

Wong, Kristin Standley, Olivia Valcarce, and everyone who helped with this book.

My critique partners—Amy Pine, Megan Erickson, Lia Riley—have always gone above and beyond in the job description. I have been blessed with an incredible group of writer friends, from Rachel Simon and Rachel Solomon, who are truly amazing and gifted writers, to the Sweet 16 author group that I've been lucky to be a part of as a debut author. A special shout-out to Darcy Woods because I can't believe you haven't always been right beside me.

And finally, to my family. A special thanks to the Cloutier family, who gave me my yearly dose of Christmas celebrations. To Josh, who is my real-life book boyfriend. And to Jonah, Micah and Toby, who are everything.

Don't miss these
delicious reads
by Suzanne Nelson!

About the Author

Natalie Blitt is the author of the young adult novel *The Distance from A to Z*. Originally from Canada, she now lives in the Chicago area with her husband and three sons, where she works at an education think tank. You can visit her online at www.natalieblitt.com.